SPLIT SCREAM

VOLUME FIVE

Featuring:

Lyndsey Croal

&

Bitter Karella

Cover illustrations by Evangeline Gallagher.

Interior illustrations by Echo Echo.

Cover and interior design by Dreadful Designs.

Edited by Alex Ebenstein.

For the ones who like it weird.

INTRODUCTION

The novelette has been dismissed and disparaged. Some dictionaries don't even define them as a unique form, listing only short stories, novellas, or novels. Others write them off as being "too sentimental" or "trivial".

This is silly, of course, and, with little effort it's easy to see the novelette has a purpose and value.

What makes a novelette, then? Exact word counts vary, but these stories are longer than a short story and shorter than a novella. In this case, between ten and twenty thousand words; or, horror you can devour in about an hour or two.

Sound like another form of storytelling?

I'm not saying a novelette is a movie is a novelette. And I'm not saying written fiction *needs* to be like movies. But... But they are *kind of* like movies in terms of length and threads, right? If you're willing to accept that premise, at least for the moment, may I present to you...

SPLIT SCREAM
A Novelette Double Feature

Truly, what better way to present these stories than as a double feature? Do you *have* to read them back to back in a single Friday night after dusk? Certainly not. But could you? Absolutely.

Shall we?

First, we get a salty taste of the sea in Lyndsey Croal's coastal curiosity, "The Girl with Barnacles for Eyes." The insidious Curator has an astonishing new feature in his traveling sideshow, and it's an exhibition where the true monsters hide in plain sight. Then, we go west to 19th century California in Bitter Karella's "The Ballad of Horse Girl." It's a classic Western tale imbued with supernatural horror, revenge from beyond the grave, and a bounty placed by Death herself.

Okay. Are you ready? Grab some popcorn, turn the lights low, and don't be afraid to scream.

This is Volume Five of SPLIT SCREAM, the series firmly rolling along now through Tenebrous Press. It's all good from here, eh?

Whether this is your first time with us, or you've read one of the previous four volumes—thanks for stopping by.

Long live the novelette!

Alex Ebenstein
Tenebrous Press
Michigan, USA
May 2024

CONTENTS

THE WONDERS BENEATH

THE GIRL WITH BARNACLES FOR EYES

Lyndsey Croal

The Girl sits still behind the glass tank, focussing on the sound of the water, steadying her breath with the flow of the bubbles rising. The Curator has told her the tank is an optical illusion, not that she really understands what that means. He tells her that to the audience it looks as though she's sitting in the water, not in a panel behind it. The audience have arrived now, their movements marked by creaking wood and muffled chatter as they board the boat to visit the Curator's exhibit.

The Curator doesn't tell her very much about her exhibit, though sometimes he tells her about the other treasures on display: trinkets from the deep and creatures like Otto the octopus, who sits in a tank in the corner of the cabin. Once, the Curator steered her through the cramped space and let her feel her way around his treasures—whale bones, metal artefacts, and glass jars which he explained are full of creatures he's captured, most of them dead now though, preserved in a strong-smelling liquid that burns her throat every time he makes a new one. The Girl doesn't like the exhibit—everything feels so cold and sharp. Otto is the exception, the only living thing here apart from her. There used to be a squid too, but during a recent docking the Curator had left the boat with the poor creature and returned without it. "Everything can be traded when the time is right," he said to her when she asked him about it, pleaded with him to bring the squid back. "It'll be good for you to remember that."

For now, the Curator has told her that of all his collection, she's his marvel, his star of the show. She is a wonder of the world to anyone who lays their eyes upon her—not that she can see why, because her eyes are now clasped shut, her vision a jagged array of greys and blacks, and rarely any light.

She has a memory, vaguely, of being able to see once. It's a faded image of the sea, lights dancing, glittering, and the sound of water, but more echoey and soft than the constant bubbling from the tank. But that magic of the water she feels can't be real—the Curator has told her about the sea's dangers, and how it can only be safe in controlled environments, where it can be contained.

Evie arrives at the exhibit just after sunrise, and still the queue stretches the length of the old pier. She can just see the façade of the crimson sail detached from the docked boat and displayed so that it looks like a curtain draped across the edge of the pier, welcoming them in. On the mast hangs a sign, *The Wonders Beneath*, written in scrawling gold lettering inlaid with shells and sparkling sea glass. The crowd is a murmur of chatter and excitement as they approach the entrance, young children bouncing on their toes to get a closer look. Above, gulls chitter and dip to observe the throng, as though hoping to join in the excitement.

The exhibit has been the talk of the town for weeks, a chance to see the dark and dangerous relics from the Curator's ocean adventures. Every midsummer, he brings back something special—strange luminescent fish, a great narwhal tusk, an octopus with super strength, and last year, a squid with ink that could reverse aging when rubbed into wrinkling skin. Evie's mum had tried it, and sure enough, her skin peeled off the very next week, leaving softer flesh beneath. She didn't tell Ma that she smelled strange for weeks after though, an awful odour coming from her skin like it was rotting from the inside out.

Evie holds her breath now as she steps under the curtain. The first exhibit has been set up in a row at the end of the pier, and the air beneath the sail is thick with the smells of the crowd and the exhibit's strange attractions. She pinches her nose as she moves onward, past jars of dead and pickled sea creatures preserved in vinegar and brine. Then, stepping over the gangway, a row of bones from the deep have been arranged—whale skulls, shark teeth, and sharpened tusks. Some are bigger than she is, and a few of the young kids even try to climb the skeletons, hiding inside grand ribs and jaws. Evie wants to study the bones, count the parts, figure out what the whale would look like put back together. She takes her notebook out, making a quick sketch, soft lines and round shapes. She imagines swimming next to the bone whale out in the ocean, far from home, as she traces her hand along the jaw line, smooth as silk.

She lingers there for as long as she dares—thinking of Ma back home—before heading inside to the main cabin. The room is smaller than she remembers, split in two parts with a curtain draped across the wooden beam in the centre. The first section is more of a living space than an exhibit, with a small futon on one side and bookshelves lining the other. Beneath the futon, there's a heavy chain coiled up with dark marks staining the ground around it. Then, in the far corner she notices the small tank, housing the octopus from a couple of years ago. Last time, the Curator had the creature in a big tank up front as the main event—had him opening sealed jars and breaking rocks apart, to show his strength. But this year, he appears smaller, no longer swimming and changing colour animatedly. Instead he is grey and faded, limbs curled up beneath him, pushing into the corner of his tank. Evie puts her hand on the glass gently. She's read that octopuses are intelligent, have emotions. If that's true, then this octopus must be lonely. She understands what that's like.

She wishes she could reach in and release him—surely, he'd be happier back in the water where he came from? Maybe he even has a family. Not that that always makes things easier, but at least in the sea he could find somewhere with more space to stretch his limbs, more places to visit, more to see than the gawping mouths of children. Here he's cramped and alone, with not even the squid remaining as company. She wonders what happened to it. Though at least Ma won't smell so bad after this year's visit.

Feeling the draw of the grand finale of the Curator's latest find, she says a quiet goodbye to the sad octopus, and continues towards the end of the cabin. Evie's stomach clenches in anticipation as she passes under the worn red velvet curtains and wooden beam arch.

A sharp breath escapes her. Whatever she'd expected to see, it wasn't this. The tank from last year remains, but at the bottom of it sits a girl. It almost looks as though she's glowing, with her silver hair twisted in a net of seaweed and kelp. She's sitting cross-legged, hands clasped in her lap.

She could just be another young woman, like Evie, if not for her strange gaze.

Clusters of barnacles line her eye sockets—closed tight, but not unmoving. Where her eyes should be, there are instead barnacles.

The Curator told the Girl that he found her alone on the shore one day, helpless after being washed up by a storm. She can't remember it though. She can't remember much beyond waking and finding herself on the stinking hard wooden floor of the boat. But he saved her, he says, and now she owes him—she has to earn her keep on this boat, and that means being a part of his exhibit.

For what feels like endless days, they travel here and there, from town to town, always on the water, but never in it. Sometimes he lets her dip her hands in the waves on a quiet day, let's her touch the cold sting of the sea. It's like ice on her fingers, but she always tries to keep her hands in for as long as possible until it feels like her fingers could almost be welded together. Then the Curator comes and pulls her away, wraps her hands in towels until she's warm again, warning her that the sea is too dangerous for feeble young women like herself, that she must never go in it again. That's how she lost her sight after all, and her memories—the ice-cold water and the waves and the storm. "The sea is a dangerous beast, Girl," the Curator had said. "No matter how much you may wish to tame it."

Now the Girl must sit still in the back of the boat, behind the echoey tank, as the audience arrives. There's a loud tap on the glass and it rings out with a sharp echo, hurting her ears. She can feel the vibrations of footsteps all around her too, and her heart is beating fast. She lifts her hands to cover her ears and starts to hum in an attempt to drown out the sounds. It helps a little, until a louder, agitated, *thud-thud* hits the glass again, reverberates like a siren.

Evie stands and stares at the Girl with barnacles for eyes. At one point, a boy beside her bangs loudly on the tank, and the Girl flinches and lifts her hands to her ears.

Evie gives him a look, and he sticks his tongue out. Ten seconds later he does it again.

Evie wonders if the Girl's ears are different too, but her silver hair hides most of her other features. Though, her fingers look wrong, somehow. Calloused and narrow, and spindly like the cold and sharp bones in the other exhibit. Evie tries to get a better look at the Girl, tries to figure out how she's breathing underwater—does she have gills, or can she breathe through her barnacle eyes? There are no bubbles coming from anywhere Evie can see. But before she can examine the Girl closer, the Curator approaches her.

"Like what you see?" he asks, so close she can smell his breath.

She steps away from the tank, shoulders tensed. "She's…" But her throat is tightening, her skin prickling at the Curator's gaze, a hard stare as though she's one of his wonders from the deep.

After a moment, he straightens and chuckles. "Another treasure for you," he says, then from his pocket he pulls out a round shell and holds it out to Evie, his fingers uncurling one by one like he's revealing a magic trick. "As beautiful as its recipient."

Evie doesn't want it, but she knows better than to refuse something from men like this. So, she takes it and whispers a quick thank you, even though the sight of him and his smile that seems to split his face in two, makes her insides squirm.

Then, with a final glance at the Girl with barnacles for eyes, she leaves the boat, hurrying out of the cabin, onto the gangway, and past the dwindling crowds. *Dwindling,* which means it must be later than she thought. Ma will be angry.

She hurries back home, and as she arrives breathless at the path, hoping Ma might not be back yet from deliveries, the door opens, and Ma steps out.

"Where have you been all day?"

Evie flinches. "I was at the exhibit," she explains. "The queue was long today."

"Was it worth it?"

The question feels like a trap. "It was… I shouldn't have stayed so long, I'm sorry."

"No," Ma says, clicking her tongue. "Heard he's got a monster locked up this year, that true?"

"She's not a monster, she's…" But Evie can't find the words. Even as she thinks about the Girl, she can't help but want to know more about her, to piece together the parts of her story, understand how she came to be how she was. Is she real or an illusion?

"Whatever *she* is, I think you should stay away from that boat this year, understand?"

"But Ma—"

"No *buts*." Ma opens the door behind her so hard it rattles on its hinges, and beckons Evie inside. "You're too old for circuses and tricks. It's time you grew up."

"But shouldn't we help her?" she says, her voice weak. "The Girl, in the tank."

Ma looks at Evie for a long moment, and Evie thinks she's about to slap her. But then she shakes her head. "This family has had enough trouble as it is. We're not getting involved, hear me?"

Evie begins to protest, but Ma pulls her inside. "Upstairs, now. And tomorrow, you can be up early in the kitchen, we've got lots of extra orders with the exhibit in town."

Evie sighs. "Yes, Ma," she says, and heads upstairs before Ma can pile on more work.

In her room, Evie sits on her bed and stares at the wall. She thinks about the tank, and the Girl, trapped there with that awful man. It's not right—she must be about the same age as Evie, sixteen or seventeen, almost grown up, and he's keeping her there like some pet. Or a trinket.

Evie walks across to her desk and pulls open the drawer. It's full of trinkets of her own she's collected from beaches—pebbles, shells, sea glass, driftwood, and other lost and broken things. Sometimes she likes to draw them, mark their form, every crevice and imperfection, on the paper. She likes how she could draw a hundred shells, and none would look the same. She takes the one the Curator gave her from her pocket. Even though she can tell it's beautiful, with mother of pearl edges and soft intricate patterns, something about it is all wrong.

As beautiful as its recipient.

The Curator's words bring another wave of discomfort. As soon as she's by the harbour again, she'll throw the shell straight in the water, deep down where it belongs.

The Curator was happy with the Girl today—told her that her performance was perfect, even though she only sat there behind the echoing glass while trying to think of anything but the loud grating noises around her. Tried not to imagine how many could see her, when she couldn't see them.

He brought her hot chips soaked in vinegar and salt for dinner as a reward, though. She's never tasted anything so delicious, but now she feels the inside of her mouth and cheeks stinging and stiff from the tanginess. He didn't give her any water to drink after, even when she asked for some, and now he's getting ready to leave her, like he often does when they're docked. Usually, he comes back loudly clunking on the boat, stinking of wine and smoke, collapsing on the futon in the main cabin, not even making it to his own quarters.

She stays quiet as the Curator gathers his things, loudly—trinkets and treasures clanking in his bag. She hopes he doesn't take Otto with him. She'd given the octopus that name. A name given, even if she doesn't have one herself, or remember what it might be. The Curator just calls her Girl or Sweetheart. The latter makes her skin crawl, the way his voice curls the syllables like he's savouring the taste of them.

She waits patiently for him to leave. At first, she thinks he might have forgotten the chain, but just as he's heading for the door, he returns to pull her to the futon and loop it around her ankle. The chain is long enough that she can venture around the space, but not long enough to go outside. *For her own protection*, or so the Curator tells her.

Once he's gone, locking the door behind him, she finds her way to Otto's tank. The chain drags in a rattle behind her as the metal links hit the ridges of the floorboards, like an anchor being drawn up from the sea. Her chain is seven steps long, and Otto is six steps from the futon—she can find her way there by the sound alone. Standing on tiptoes at the edge of his tank, she dips her hand in until she feels the water move. Otto is still there, and he stretches out a limb to greet her, gently places it on her own.

"I wish I could see you," she says. She has an image in her mind of what he looks like, of his colours changing as he swims, playing, alongside her. Has she imagined it or seen it before? "I wish you could be free."

Otto squeezes her hand in response, then dips and swims around her arm as she moves it in the water. It's soothing, and she wishes the tank was big enough for her to climb inside, big enough to swim with him like she sees in her mind. She tried once to open up the show tank, but it was sealed shut and she wasn't able to find any latch. Now the Curator has her chained up tighter, so she can no longer reach it. Maybe the Curator is worried she'd drown if she got in. The Girl wonders if she could swim if she tried, like Otto does, or if she'd simply sink to the bottom. For now at least she takes comfort in the octopus's company, speaking to him, asking him questions, and waiting for the squeezes in response. Somehow, she feels like he can understand her, that he is communicating with her in his own way, each reassuring one another. Captivity is their shared connection. Maybe that's why he puts up with her. He cowers away from the Curator when he tries to coax the poor creature from his corner spot with curses and harsh words. The tank used to have rocks and plants where Otto could sit and hide, but the Curator has moved them now, so all she feels inside the glass is empty, echoey, space.

Evie can't stop thinking about the Girl—her silver ethereal hair, the way her barnacle eyes pulsed ever so slightly as they moved in her direction. The way her expression looked thoughtful but sad. But Ma won't let her visit again, nor give her the coin needed for the visiting fee. So, when Ma sends her out for her deliveries the next afternoon, arms full of breads and oatcakes from the bakery, she sprints to finish the tasks in half the time. Then she sneaks a coin from her payment—just a small amount, so Ma shouldn't notice—and wanders down to the harbour. At the edge of the old pier on her way to the boat, she stops for a moment. As the waves slosh against the sea-blackened beams, she takes out the shell from the Curator and throws it into the sea. In the air its bright rainbow colours reflect in the sunlight before it sinks into the grey water, its beauty to be lost to the sand. At least it's free from the Curator's collection, now. She turns her attention back to the boat, and heads onwards to the exhibit.

She rushes past the first parts of it, the jars of dead things and bones, and the octopus who looks almost dead himself, towards the final exhibit at the back of the boat. She stands by the tank longer this time, looking in at the Girl with barnacles for eyes. She stays as quiet as possible as the rest of the crowd mill in and out, the Curator in the corner taking their money and their praise, watching her closely. When the last of the crowd has been and gone, Evie sneaks closer to the tank and puts her ear against it. There's a sound coming from somewhere. A soft humming. The Girl is singing, she realises, a gentle tune, muffled as though heard through a shell. But somehow, it's the most beautiful sound she's ever heard, and she feels as though she could swim in it forever.

"Back again?" the Curator says suddenly, pulling her from the reverie. His eyes narrow. "Like the exhibit, do you?"

"It's beautiful," Evie says, looking now at the Girl.

"Aye, that she is."

"No, I mean the song."

"What song?" the Curator asks with a twitch of his thick grey brow.

"You can't hear it?"

"All I can hear right now is the sound of merriment at the Shingle Inn that I'm currently missing," he says, stepping towards her, wafting the smell of wine and sweat in her direction. "Which would be okay, I suppose, if there was something else to entertain me."

Evie stands up, eyes darting between the Girl and the door. "I should get home," she says, and moves to the door. "My Ma will be expecting me back."

"That'll be an extra coin before you go," he says. "You stayed twice as long as anyone else."

Evie starts to panic. "That's not… I don't have any…"

He eyes her belt. "The coin purse there looks pretty full to me."

"It's not mine," she says. "Please, she'll notice."

He barks out a laugh. "Ah, I see… We could keep it our little secret if you like," he says. "Find another way to pay for it."

She doesn't like the look he gives her, how his eyes are tracing every inch of her body. She feels suddenly exposed, and stupid for staying so long. Steadying her breath, she reaches to her coin purse and holds one out to him. He tilts his hat out and takes the extra coin, but doesn't step aside straight away. The Curator simply watches her, flicking a coin between his fingers. Then, after a few long seconds of staring her down, he shifts to the side barely enough to let her squeeze past. Still, as she leaves, he's so close to her that his hand brushes against her back and she feels a sudden coldness, like she's been doused in water. Evie glances briefly at the Girl in the tank, who she swears is now following her movement as she leaves. Evie runs—off the boat, off the gangway, and down the old pier, ignoring any looks she gets from the other townsfolk.

Ma is waiting for her back home again, arms sharp on her hips. "Where were you?"

Evie's eyes dart back to the sea automatically. "Deliveries," she says, trying to keep any wavering from her voice.

"That's funny," Ma says. "Because, I was just at Miriam's, the last place on your list. Went to see if you'd got lost, and she says you delivered the bread hours ago. So the next thing you tell me better well be the truth."

Evie's stomach sinks. "I…I just went for a walk after finishing the deliveries. Lost track of time."

Ma hisses a *tsk* and steps closer. "I know you went to the boat. Mr Abbot saw you."

Evie has to work hard not to roll her eyes—Mr Abbot, the old man from down the way, always meddling, as though his sole purpose in life was to make everyone else miserable because he had nothing else better to do. "He's lying."

Ma frowns. "Takings for today, then?"

Evie takes out the coin purse, heart beating too fast. "Here," she says, passing it over.

Ma tilts the coin into her hands, counts them one by one, and Evie is reminded of the Curator, the way his fingers moved with the coins, like they're one and the same. Her face twists into a smile as she reaches the end of the count. "I suppose the missing money just leapt out of your purse and wandered away?"

Evie opens her mouth then closes it quickly, like a drowning fish.

"I assume that's how you paid for your entry?"

Ma steps closer, and Evie pushes herself back against the kitchen counter. "I don't know what you mean."

"I'm not stupid, Evie," she says. "I know you went to that boat."

"Ma…I'm sorry, but…it's just, it's not right, the Girl, we have to help her."

"We'll do no such thing."

"She doesn't want to be there."

"Did she tell you that?"

"No, I…I can just tell."

"And if we did go and *'help her'* what do you propose we do after?" she says. "I can barely afford to keep you, never mind some freak of nature."

Evie feels a twist in her stomach. "She's not a freak. She's amazing, and beautiful."

"You're not to go back to see her," Ma says. "And if I find you stealing from me again, you will regret it. You don't want to become like your father, do you? He was a liar and a waste of space too."

Evie shrinks, thinking of the day Ma broke the news to her that Pa had left and was never coming back. It had never made any sense to her, how he could leave her like that. Ma was still putting everything from the bakery sales toward paying off his gambling debts, with Evie forced to help, even though she'd rather be doing anything else. "No, Ma."

"Then go, get out of my sight, and think about how you can make up for this."

It's the middle of the night and Evie can't sleep. Ma locked her door from the outside, but had not locked the window, so Evie hooks her feet into the trellis trailing up the cottage and climbs down. It's been a couple of years since she's had to do it, and she worries it'll break under her weight. Then Ma would be there to deliver much worse than being locked in a room. But it holds. With the last jump, she lands heavily into the shrubbery below and rolls her ankle. She bites down on her lip to stop herself from crying out and leans back into the wall, waiting to see if a candle flickers to life from above. Thankfully, all remains dark in the cottage.

She pulls her coat over her head and tiptoes away from the house, onto the quiet cobbled streets, and towards the pier. The last of the night's revellers have just left the Shingle Inn, and Evie notices a tall, cloaked man striding away from it. The Curator, heading back to his boat. There's no light on the boat and Evie wonders if the Girl is there all by herself. She doesn't like the idea of it—how alone she must feel when she's on her own, how awful it must be when the Curator is there. It's no kind of life to lead, trapped like that, between such dismal options.

Evie looks beyond the red sails to the sea behind, the darkness of it sharp as a knife, almost blending into the starlit sky. Since Pa left, she often imagines sneaking her way onto a trading boat and simply sailing away from here. Leaving this nowhere town, leaving Ma, and Pa's gambling debt, and every other miserable thing behind. She could get a job on a crew somewhere—she's learned enough about seafaring from when she and Pa used to take their own fishing boat out, and she's always been good with her hands. She can tie knots, draw maps—maybe she could even become a merchant, sell wares and art like the eccentric woman from one of the inland towns that visits here in midsummer. Then she could have a new life, in a place that didn't smell of dead fish and misery.

She glances at the pier, half expecting to see a boat sail into port and Pa stepping off, returning from a long voyage, saying he never meant to be away for so long, that he never meant to leave her. He would bring a bag full of treasures and take her away from here. But of course, the horizon remains dark and empty.

Pa's fishing boat was the first thing Ma sold after he was gone, and Evie has never forgiven her for it, just like she's never forgiven Pa for leaving in the first place. She imagines him sometimes, on a trader boat faraway, on his own adventures without them—why couldn't he have just taken her with him?

The Girl's hands are numb, too long spent playing with Otto, and she can feel her fingers almost stuck together. As she warms them in a blanket, she perches on the windowsill next to the futon nook, leans her head against it so she can feel the slither of the breeze that slips in from the outside. It won't be long until the Curator returns. She hopes he'll have made lots of coin, then at least he'll be in a good mood. At the last town, he came back one night, yelling about townsfolk with no taste. He yelled at her and threw things about the cabin. He even broke a couple of his jars of dead things. The smell of it wasn't even the worst part—she'd stepped on a shard of glass the next day and had to take care to tread softly days after. The

Curator spent that day on deck drinking away his sorrows, leaving her to pick up and discard the remaining glass. Her foot felt raw for weeks, and even now, the scar has healed awkwardly, leaving a sharp line in the base of her heel that feels like rubber.

After that first night of watching the boat, once Ma has gone to bed, Evie continues to sneak out her window and down to the pier. She starts to spend sleepless nights, wrapped in a blanket and scarf, hidden behind a stack of crab creels, watching the boat and looking out for the Curator. She's worked out that he always follows the same pattern: he leaves the boat, locks it up, and heads to the Shingle Inn at the harbour with a bag full to bursting that jingles and clinks with his trinkets. The Inn is where all the locals drink—where Evie's Pa used to drink too.

One night, instead of waiting by the pier, Evie sneaks out towards the Inn and lurks outside the window, peering inside. It's not a place she's supposed to be—not a place ordinarily for women, never mind young ones like her. But she can't help wanting to see what the Curator is doing. The Inn is as busy as it always is on an evening, and the Curator sits at a table in the centre, showing off his wares. He appears to be putting on a performance, telling tales she can't quite hear as he holds each item up animatedly. Occasionally there are laughs and cheers, then later, when the ale and wine have taken hold, he takes off his sea captain's hat and shakes the coin and other payments from the patrons. It's after midnight when he leaves the Inn, and he stops to speak to Murdo, the owner, on his way out. They linger in the doorway as the Curator passes a handful of glinting coins to Murdo under torchlight, and the owner pockets them quickly before heading back inside. Then the Curator zigzags, with pockets fuller than when he arrived back to the boat.

The Girl has been counting the days in this town in her mind. Seven exhibit days so far. The longest they've ever stayed in one town is fourteen days, though sometimes they stay no longer than six. She wonders what it is about her that makes the audience keep coming. Is it to do with the tank she has to sit behind, the water bubbling around her? She has asked the Curator before, but he only tells her she is a treasure, and greedy townsfolk like treasure. That's why she has to be locked up too, so no one would be tempted to steal her away.

The Girl has noticed that they usually leave after the crowds slow, after the magic of their exhibit fades—after they run out of coin to pay the Curator with. How long will it take for this town to grow bored of her? And then she finds darker thoughts drift into her mind. What will happen when all the towns have seen the exhibit? How long until the Curator decides he needs a new treasure for his show? Will he sell her away once she's no longer a novelty, like the squid?

Everything can be traded when the time is right.

After a week of watching the Curator's movements, Evie finally gathers the courage to visit the boat—she'll wait for the Curator to leave, then she'll sneak onboard and find a way to speak to the Girl, to help her. Taking a deep breath, she opens the window quietly, and climbs down the trellis. But then, as she's halfway, the trellis unhooks from the wall and breaks. She falls backwards into the sharp grasses beneath. At least the sandy soil offers some cushion, and she lands almost noiselessly. But now she won't be able to sneak back this way. She'll have to creep through the front door. Though that will have to be a problem in a few hours. Or maybe, the thought crosses her mind, she won't have to come back. Maybe, when the Curator is away, she could simply take the boat and sail away. He was often away for a few hours. Long enough. Why hadn't the thought come before when she could have brought more supplies with her?

The thrill of the idea in her mind, she runs down to the pier, pulling her scarf around her face. She's worn the darkest garments too, in case anyone spots her from a distance—she doesn't want Mr Abbot or anyone else warning Ma about her nighttime adventures.

At the edge of the pier, adrenaline buzzing in her ears, she waits wearily for the lanterns to go out on the boat. For the Curator to leave. But something is wrong as soon as he steps onto the gangway. He's not alone. He's brought the

Girl with barnacles for eyes with him. Evie holds her breath and skulks into the shadows, hiding behind a stack of shipment crates to watch.

The Girl looks different on land—slight and thin, her skin grey and pallid in the moonlight. The Curator holds her arm as he leads her, and she walks with disjointed steps, tripping occasionally on the uneven boards of the pier. Evie steps back as they get closer, crouches further into darkness, and knocks a pebble off the side in the process. It splashes in the water behind, and though Evie thought it was too quiet to hear, the Girl with barnacles for eyes jolts round and stares. Can the Girl see her?

The Curator stops too, gives the Girl a tug. "What's wrong?"

"Nothing," the Girl says, her voice gentle, but strained. "I only heard something in the sea."

"At least some of your senses are working," he says, then he pulls her along again.

"I don't want to go further away," she says suddenly, her voice rising in a rasp as though she's about to scream. "I don't want to go so far from the sea. I *can't*."

The Curator looks at her, tipping his hat up slightly, pushing his greasy fringe out of his eyes. "You'll be fine," he says, and tugs her hard. It looks like the Girl is trying to resist, but she's too weak for him and she can't help but continue with him along the pier, her gait still uneven, as if she's unused to walking. Evie feels an anger build inside her—the way he speaks to her, the way he tugs at the Girl like she's nothing. It's the same way Ma speaks to her.

As they continue away from the harbour, Evie follows from a distance. Every so often, the Girl with barnacle for eyes turns to glance over her shoulder, and every time, Evie hides in the shadows.

The Girl is so sure she heard something, so sure of the footsteps behind her. She doesn't tell the Curator—he wouldn't listen anyway, and she's not sure she wants him to know.

There was someone else on the pier, and they were watching.

The thought of it is quickly quashed from her mind as a door is flung open and she's pulled inside a new space by the Curator. The sound is so loud the Girl can hardly bear it. The smell too—a thick scent that cloys at her throat, makes her feel sick, worse than the odour of the Curator's cigars that he smokes during longer voyages.

As she walks with the Curator, his grip hard on her arm, she feels other hands on her, grabbing at her as she passes, pinching at her skin, tugging at her hair.

"Get that freak out of here," a voice cries from a distance, and footsteps approach. A large body is blocking their way, one that smells of fried meat and oil. The Curator pushes her behind him, still holding her tight. She can feel her arm bruising, and she worries if he squeezes any harder her bones might break.

"Come now Murdo, no need for all that, she's a part of my collection," he whispers. "You've had no issue with my other treasures."

She hears the man called Murdo whisper a curse under his breath. "You'll scare away my customers with whatever nonsense you've planned," he says, the words almost drowned out by the drone of the merriment and music around them. A jarring concoction of noises and voices.

"Well, how about I cut you in on the profits?" the Curator says. "A silver for every gold I make. And if it goes badly, I promise not to take her here again."

A pause then. "*Two* silvers."

"We have a deal my friend," the Curator says, and it sounds like he slaps the other man on the back. Then he clears his throat. "Good evening, fine folk!" His voice booms, commanding the attention of the room. "Two silvers, and the Girl will grant you luck at sea," he says. "One gold, and I will ask her to look into the future, tell you what it holds."

A hush falls over the bar. The music stops, and she wonders if the Curator has made a misstep. If they're about to be chased from here. Then a set of footsteps approach.

"We're off to sea tomorrow, a whaling trip," the new man says. "Could do with some luck for the voyage."

"Aye," the Curator says. "That she can do. How many sailors are there?"

"Four of us here," the voice says. "But we're not paying eight silvers."

"Why don't we do you a deal, then, three for the price of four?"

There's a pause, then the sound of coins being passed around, and she can almost feel the hunger of the Curator as he takes the coins. Even though he knows she cannot grant luck—if she could, she would have brought some for herself, to get away from the Curator, and away from his boat.

"How does it work exactly," the seafaring man says.

"Come, let's sit."

The Curator drags her to a stool and pushes her onto it. The presence of the men around her feels suffocating, all clearly more than twice her size. Panic rises in her gut, bile in the back of her throat, and she wonders if this is what drowning feels like. She tries to think of the water instead, of the sea and its sounds, to calm her, but it's almost impossible in the drone of the Inn.

"Now," the Curator says, and he takes something from his bag, places it on the table in front of her, then guides her hands to it. It's a round object, made of glass, cold as ice.

"This is a storm glass," the Curator says to the gathered crowd, which the Girl can feel is growing steadily, to watch whatever it is the Curator will have her do. "The Girl will look into it and direct the weather for your voyage."

The Curator leans over suddenly and hisses in her ear so only she can hear. "Tell them their trip will go well and make it convincing."

The Girl takes a deep breath and grips the glass tight. She tilts her head to the side and imagines the men and their boat out on water, tries to find the words of safe passage and good weather. But instead another image fills her mind. Figures aboard a great vessel, sails unfurling, waves crashing over the bow so hard they splinter the ship in half. It sinks, and there are screams, shouts. The figures fall one by one into the cold depths of the sea, and in her vision, she is waiting beneath, eyes finally open under the water to see it all unfold. She is smiling, so wide her mouth cracks into a gaping maw. She swallows the ship and the men whole, then she swims back down to the depths, singing of her victory.

She lets out a sharp breath, and there's a mumble of voices around her.

"What did you see?" one of the men asks.

She's unsure where the image came from and knows she can't tell that version of the story if she wants to leave this Inn safely. Still, she thinks on it with a certain satisfaction as she opens her mouth to tell the lie of an easy journey.

But she doesn't get a chance to start. A yell comes from behind, followed by a commotion and rumble of conversation. There's a clatter, and someone, a higher-pitched voice she thinks she's heard before, is screaming out.

"Murdo!" a voice shouts. "Look what I found outside, a filthy rat, lurking by the back door. Bet she had a mind to steal something. Runs in the blood, I'd say."

Evie feels like her scalp is going to be ripped off as Chef Hansen pulls her inside by the hair. She had been trying to sneak into the Inn unseen, to see the Girl and what the Curator was up to, but as she rounded the back door, Hansen came out to empty a pot of scraps and caught her in the act. She tried to run, but Hansen grabbed her straight away and dragged her inside.

She tilts her neck as best she can, as all the eyes in the Inn follow her movements, some with smiles and subdued laughter as if the whole thing is amusing, others with looks as though she's dirt on their shoes.

Hansen throws her at Murdo's feet, and when she tries to stand, he kicks her in the gut so that she falls, hunched over in pain. She can't breathe for a few seconds, and she coughs, splutters. Hansen makes to hit her again with the back of his hand, but another man intervenes and grabs it.

"That's enough," he says to Hansen. Evie recognises him as Ally, one of Pa's old fisher friends. He used to visit when she was younger, with his own daughter, Orla. The poor girl died of a fever when she was ten, and Evie had barely seen Ally since. He looks older than he should now, haggard. But his eyes are kind.

"She's just a girl," he adds when Hansen doesn't let go.

"Aye, well she's old enough to steal, so she's old enough to pay the consequences," Hansen says.

"I wasn't stealing," Evie croaks.

Murdo crouches down to her as Ally watches them closely. "Explain why you were sneaking about outside the Inn after your bedtime then." He speaks to her like she's a child, while still leering at her with narrowed eyes and a smirk.

Evie looks around, and her eyes fall on the middle of the Inn where the Curator is now standing and staring at her. Next to him sits the Girl with barnacles for eyes. She appears to be looking at Evie in her own way, barnacle eyes moving without opening, her mouth forming an 'O'. The Curator arranged her meticulously to bring her here: draped kelp across her shoulders, gently tousled her hair with salt water, and adorned her skin with stripes of shimmering squid ink. In front of her is a glass globe with splintered frost up the sides—it's like the old storm glass Pa used to keep in the house, to predict the weather. If Evie is remembering correctly, it's showing there's a storm coming.

The Curator steps towards them. "Ach, this may be all my fault," he says suddenly. "I think I might have encouraged this girl the other day, at the exhibit." He strides over, dragging the Girl up to follow. "She's enamoured by me, you see, by my trinkets and treasures. And who can blame her?" He puffs out his chest.

Beside her, Ally stifles a laugh, and the Curator throws him a look.

"That true?" Murdo asks Evie in his gruff voice, and as the Curator stares at her with his dark sharp eyes, she gives a single nod.

"Still, for the trouble of it, I think you and your Ma can spare a few extra deliveries this week, no charge."

"But I didn't—"

"I'll take her home," Ally says, helping her stand. "And I'm sure the deliveries can be arranged." He locks eyes with Murdo for a long moment before the Inn owner gives a sly grin.

"As you were," Murdo says, then she leans down and ruffles Evie's hair like she's an animal. "Good girl."

Evie feels sick, but she lets Ally steer her out of the Inn, all eyes on her as she walks helplessly out. Even the Girl has her barnacle eyes on her, though her shoulders are slumped low, her body appearing deflated.

"You need to be more careful, Evie," Ally says as he walks her home.

"But I didn't do anything, I just wanted…" But she doesn't finish, because she's not really sure what she wanted. What did she expect, sneaking into the Inn like that after dark? Did she think she was going to be able to get to the Girl and rescue her somehow? She'd been foolhardy and now she was going to pay for it.

Ally watches her for a moment, then he sighs. "Your Pa got on the wrong side of some folks too, you know," he says. "But he never deserved what happened to him."

She turns to him. "What do you mean?"

"You know why he left?"

"Ma says he had a gambling debt, that he stowed away on a trader ship, and ran off."

Ally stops and catches her gaze. "No, Evie," he says, a pained look on his face. "Your Ma…she was the one with the debt. Kept taking out loans, ended up in debt to Hugo and his company, and wasn't able to pay it back."

Evie feels like her legs are wobbling beneath her. "Hugo, from the shipyard?"

Ally gave a nod. "Your Pa tried to talk him into forgiving it, but the only way he'd agree was if your Pa joined up on one of his trader ships for a season, pay it off with service." He pauses to take a breath, as if deciding whether he ought to tell the rest of the tale.

Evie moves her hand to her ear, where the silver sea glass earrings Pa had given her just before he left still hang. She clutches one tight, feels the cold smooth surface of the glass as she asks a question she's almost afraid to hear the answer to. "What happened to him?"

Ally shakes his head. "The ship came back without him." He sighs again. "Some of the men said he fell overboard, others said he was driven to madness by the dark and cold, and jumped. They never found his…they never found him. I'm sorry, Evie. I thought you knew. Your Pa, he was a good man."

Evie suddenly feels small. She doesn't know what situation is worse—that Pa might have jumped into the sea, or that Ma had lied about it for the last five years. Did they even still have a debt to pay off? Could he still be alive somewhere? Or was he simply dead and bloated, under the deep dark sea? All the questions swirl in her mind, sharp and cold.

"Thank you for telling me," she says.

"I'm sorry I was the first one that did."

She gives a nod as they round the corner to the cottage. Ma's lantern is lit—she won't be able to climb up the window to her room. And if Ma's up, the front door isn't going to be an option.

"Don't tell her about the Inn," she says to Ally quickly. "Please."

He sighs. "You tell her what you want, Evie, just…be more careful next time." As he makes to leave, he puts a hand on her shoulder, his face etched with worry lines. "You'd do well to stay out of the Curator's way, too. That man, he's a wrong sort. And he seems to have eyes for you. So you'd be best to keep out his sight."

She nods. "Thank you, for…."

He waves a hand and gives her a sad smile. This time he does leave, and heads up the hill away from town, in the direction of the cemetery, on his way to no doubt visit his daughter.

As she opens the garden gate, Ma comes striding out with eyes like fire. Evie takes a deep breath and prepares to take the wrath again.

As the Girl with barnacles for eyes sits in the Inn, she thinks about the other girl's voice from before—the way it rose and lilted, soft as a wave, even as she was being beaten and was fighting for herself. She thinks of the way the Curator spoke to the other girl, his voice sugar-sweet, and dangerous. She ponders all of this as she's steered from group to group, to give her readings for the folks in the Inn. Some want to be brought good fortune on travels, some desire riches, while others want her to grant them luck with romance. She knows she can deliver on none of their requests, but that if she doesn't at least pretend, it'll be worse for her when the Curator takes her back to the boat. Her guilt about the lies lessens though, as she continues with the readings—she hates the way the other folks speak to her, voices sharp and demanding, some prodding at her or tugging at her hair as though taking strands of it will bring extra luck. It's worse than in the exhibit. Here she feels exposed and out of her depth in a different way. At least in the tank, she has the illusion of distance, of being untouchable. Now, all she can think about is getting back to the boat so she can be closer to the sea again. Something tells her she's never been this far on land. What kind of a life does she have, that her greatest current wish is to be back in her usual imprisonment?

By the time they leave the Inn, the Girl feels folded in, like her body has been stretched and bruised. She feels the ache of it deep in her bones, as her head buzzes with tinny sounds from the loudness of the Inn.

The Curator is drunk, but in good spirits, his grip lighter than usual. For a moment, she thinks about trying to push him over, trying to run away, but where would she go? And she realises with a strange ache, that she doesn't know what she'd do without him. She's in an unfamiliar world with no memories, no way of earning a living, no way of finding food, or shelter. Maybe she could push him over and jump into the sea and swim and swim, until she found somewhere new or drowned in the process. Just as she's considering the option, the Curator's grip tightens around her arm and the sound of the boat comes into earshot, the creaking of the mast, the whisper of the sails like a hush of conspiring voices.

He pulls her into the main cabin and drunkenly chains her to her futon, then he stumbles out the door, locking it behind. Her dreams of freedom are quelled. Except, when she leans down to check the ankle hold, she finds he's not clicked the second bolt into the chain. He must have been too drunk to notice. She squeezes at the first bolt with her fingers, tries to loosen it. It's jammed in tight, but maybe with the other bolt loosened, there's enough movement to wiggle free. As she's pulling at it, careful to make as little sound as possible, another image floods into her mind like before. She's out on the water next to the boat, moving and swimming with the waves. Otto darts beside her, free and flashing with many colours. And in that image, there's someone else on the deck—the silhouette of a young woman with dark curly hair at the helm, a map in one hand. The vision gradually fades from her mind, but she tries to hold onto that image of freedom—the sea, the brightness, and another girl like her on the boat, without any sign of the Curator at all.

After yelling at her for sneaking out and for being the talk of the town, Evie's Ma locks her in her room and doesn't let her out the next morning. She even has the window boarded over, so only a sliver of daylight comes through. Then, Ma leaves her in the house alone, and Evie loses track of time. She tries prying at the wood, but all she gains are a few splinters and broken, bleeding nails.

She finds herself thinking of the Girl again, confined and captive, just like she is. She wonders if the Girl too dreams of escaping, of taking to the open sea and never returning. She sits at her desk, and in the dim light she takes out her notebook and she starts to draw the Girl as best she can. Beside the portrait, she draws things from the exhibit too—the sad octopus, the hollow bones, the jars full of dead and bloated things. After, Evie examines her work. The Girl's cluster of eyes aren't quite right. She drew them so carefully, matching the image she has in her mind, yet they look wrong. As though they should be open, looking at her, seeing her for the first time.

She hears the slam of the door downstairs and quickly rolls up the drawing and pockets it. Ma comes marching up the stairs, unlocks the door.

"Outside," she says. "You're helping me with deliveries this afternoon."

Evie doesn't argue and heads out. She waits in the garden as Ma gathers what she needs from the house, returning with two satchels over her shoulder. Evie offers to help, but Ma pushes her away. "Just walk," she says.

In silence, she follows Ma dutifully. They head to the Shingle Inn first, delivering one of the satchels, full of loaves, double what Murdo usually takes.

"For the trouble of last night," Ma says.

Murdo takes them and tilts his chin to Evie. "Best keep your girl away from here in the future."

Ma smiles. "No need to worry about that," she says. "I've got it handled."

Murdo gives Evie a look she doesn't like, then Ma turns and heads towards the pier. Towards the Curator's boat.

"Where are we going?"

Ma doesn't answer. But it's clear they're headed to the exhibit. There's a sign hanging across it that it's closed today, and Evie wonders if that means the boat is soon to leave town. She feels a tug of both relief and pain, thinking of the Girl leaving, but the Curator along with her. But then why were they here now, after Ma told her explicitly to stay away?

Evie stops at the gangway. "What are we doing?" she asks, more frantic this time.

Ma gives her a tight smile, then grabs her wrist. "Isn't this what you wanted?" Her words are sharp as nails, and Evie feels a chill at the back of her neck as Ma pulls her aboard.

They circle round the outer side to the deck where the Curator stands at the helm. From the smile he gives them it's clear they're expected. But Ma doesn't take anything from her bag to deliver. So why are they here?

Ma directs Evie to the man and pushes her to him. "She's strong, able," Ma says. "And her pa taught her seafaring, so she'll be an asset to you."

Evie turns, but Ma won't meet her gaze. "What—"

"Wheesht," she shooshes her.

The Curator is looking Evie up and down, circling her, as though she's a prize sheep at a fair. "Age?"

"Sixteen, she'll be seventeen in the Summer," Ma says.

The Curator's lip curls, then he holds out a hand to Ma. "She'll do."

Ma nods and passes the satchel over to her. "Your things. You're lucky I didn't throw them in the sea."

Evie peers inside and finds a disorganised mess of old clothes, as well as the papers, trinkets, and books from her desk. It's not much, but it's everything she's ever owned.

"Ma," she says, her voice a whisper. "Please."

Ma isn't listening. She only has eyes for the Curator, who has just pulled a pouch from his pocket. He passes it to Ma, who takes it without hesitation. Evie watches as she counts out the coins, one by one, dozens of gold coins. It's more money than Evie has ever seen, and yet it's still not enough—not enough for what Evie now realises the payment is for. Ma is selling her only daughter, for a bag of coins. Is Evie now to work on the boat or is she to be part of his exhibit? Or something more? The thought of it hits her like a harpoon in the chest and she can hardly breathe.

Ma finally looks at her, a furrow on her brow, and Evie searches for any hint of regret, of uncertainty. Then Ma puts a hand on her shoulder, like she's about to pull Evie in for a hug—and plucks the silver earrings from her ears and pockets them along with the pouch. She turns away without so much as another word.

"Ma!" she shouts. "You can't leave me with him!"

Ma stops briefly but keeps her back to Evie. "I've no use for you."

Evie sucks in a breath. "I see why Pa jumped now. To get away from you!"

Ma lets out a sharp laugh and turns, her eyes like fire. "You really think that was an accident, him falling into the sea?" She says it slowly, and the words twist in Evie's chest like a knife. "Behave yourself, or you might just find you'll be following him."

Then Ma was gone, rounding the side of the boat, her footsteps loud on the gangway.

Evie tries to chase after her, but the Curator is too fast. He grabs her arm tight and she can feel her skin pinch under his grip. He then picks up a bulk of mooring rope, loops it over his other shoulder, and drags her through the boat. She tries to fight, but the Curator is twice her size— she's no match for him as they move past the tank and into the main cabin. Inside, the Girl with barnacles for eyes is crouched down by a futon, gripping her ankle which is locked in a chain, while Evie is dragged to a wooden column opposite. The Curator pushes her against the wood, and using the mooring rope, he ties her wrists to her waist and her waist to the wooden column.

"Only temporary," he says, lightly. "Until I can trust you to behave."

"You're disgusting." She spits the words out, but he's unfazed.

"Your ma says you wanted to leave this town," he says. "You're lucky I'm so accommodating as to make your dream come true." His smile wounds her more than the rough material now digging into her skin. After he's tightened the rope, leaving no room for her to move, he leaves her there. Helpless. No matter how much she screams the Curator doesn't return, though she can hear his thudding boots echoing on the deck as he marches back and forth. She struggles and strains against the rope, but there's no way to break free. Then, the boat shudders beneath her, rocks back and forth. Her stomach flips with the motion. They've set sail. This isn't the vision she'd had in her mind when she had imagined escaping Ma and this town. Instead, she's only been thrown from one confinement into another. She leans forwards, head hanging limp, and cries. Her tears taste of salt and betrayal.

Across from her, the other Girl, her fellow captive, is facing her with barnacle eyes clasped shut. Dark and unmoving.

"It'll be okay," the Girl says after letting Evie's tears run dry. Her voice is so gentle, melodic as a song. "What is your name?"

Evie looks across at her, blinks the salt from her eyes. The boat is rocking with the waves, and Evie feels her stomach twist a little with every movement—she's never been out this far before, not even with Pa. "Evie," she says quietly.

"Evie," the Girl repeats, and it sounds so beautiful spoken by her.

"And you?" Evie asks, trying to fix her eyes on anything but the sky outside the window behind the Girl, which is moving too much for her liking.

The Girl pulls herself a little towards her, and Evie notices her ankle is raw where the chain is attached, the skin peeling away in tiny pieces like fish scales. "I don't know my name," she says, her shoulders dropping. "I don't remember."

Evie feels a tug in her chest, and she wants to reach out to the Girl, to comfort her. "I'm sorry," she says. "Maybe there's a way to find it again."

"The sea gives, and the sea takes," the Girl says, and the boat lurches like it heard her—or like they're heading into a storm. "I heard that once," the Girl continues. "In a dream, I think."

"So the sea took your name?"

The Girl looks thoughtful for the moment. "Perhaps I never had a name." Her chain keeps her a full two steps from Evie, and now she cranes her head, as if she's trying to get a better view. "What do you look like? Can you describe yourself to me?"

"I'm about your height I suppose, maybe a wee bit taller." Evie is trying to keep her breath steady, to focus on the conversation and not the coming storm, or the fact she's tied inside a boat that might sink with a single rogue wave. "And I've got brown curly hair, and green eyes, and my pa's nose. He always used to say I got it from him, anyway; it's slightly crooked, like it's been hooked by a fish." She smiles.

The Girl laughs a little. "What do I look like?"

Evie frowns, blushing as she tries to find the words. "Oh. You're…well, you have long silver hair like the moon, and your eyes are…well, they're different than mine—"

"I'm a monster," the Girl says, but her words are void of any harshness.

"No," Evie says. "You're beautiful."

The Girl is quiet for a moment, then she asks, "Can monsters not be beautiful?"

Evie considers. "I suppose," she says. "But I know you're not a monster." She leans forwards as far as the rope will let her, closer to the Girl. There's a faint smell of seaweed on the air, sweet and tangy.

"The Curator, he's a monster," the Girl says.

"Yes," Evie agrees. "Did he do this to you?"

"Do what?"

"The eyes."

Outside, the sails thrash loudly and the floorboards creak beneath them. The Girl shakes her head. "I don't remember. I only remember waking up here." She puts a hand to her face and traces it from her barnacle eyes to her ears. Evie sees that those are different too, small flaps with ridges beneath them, tracking down her neck like gills. "But I know that they're a part of me."

"Do they hurt?" Evie asks, feeling a temptation to reach out and touch them.

"They feel tight, strained. But they're not painful. Not like this." She points to her ankle, where her flaking skin now seems to glimmer like starlight.

"He has to set us loose at some point," Evie says. "Then maybe we could try to make a run for it."

"And go where?" the Girl asks.

"Anywhere."

"Anywhere," the Girl whispers. "I'd like that."

They stay quiet for a while, listening to one another's breathing and the groans of the ship. Evie looks around the rest of the room to see if there could be an easy escape route. The Curator has secured most of the exhibit items safely with leather straps and wooden boards, but the bottles and bones still rattle and thud as they're jerked from side to side with the building waves. There is a small hatch though, between the archway and the tank area—most likely storage, Evie assumes.

It soon grows dark outside, and for a while the waves lull into an uneasy calm. The small lantern in the cabin seems to be running out of oil, the flame barely a flicker, and Evie feels her eyes grow tired. How long have they been out at sea?

Just as Evie thinks the worst of the storm might be over, the rain begins. Soft at first, but quickly becoming a torrent, battering against every side of the boat. Evie's whole body tenses, and she closes her eyes, braces herself against the wooden column. But then, something beautiful breaks through the sound of the storm. Evie opens her eyes and sees the Girl is singing, the sounds rising gently with the rain, in harmony with it. Evie is mesmerised by the melody, and even as the lantern flickers out, the darkness it leaves behind isn't absolute. For in the blackness, the Girl's skin shimmers as the melody of her song wraps itself around her form.

"Beautiful," Evie whispers, too gently for the Girl to hear she thinks, but the Girl's head jerks up to look at Evie anyway.

She stops singing suddenly and puts an ear to the floorboard. "Don't you hear it?" she asks. "The sea, it sings back."

Evie is silent and the Girl waits for a response, her head pressed to the cold wood, listening to the song whirring beneath her. They are a hundred voices, singing, melodic, familiar, calling out to her. "You don't hear it?" she asks Evie again.

"No," Evie says, her voice soft. "I only heard you." A pause then. "Please, don't stop though. The song."

The Girl sits back up and is about to start singing again when the boat jerks suddenly. She's thrown sideways, flailing, and she grabs out for something to hold onto. But instead she careens into a wooden beam, stomach-first. She wheezes and rasps, tries to breathe.

"Are you okay?" Evie shouts.

The Girl pulls herself around the beam. Though she feels an ache in her ribs, she gives a small nod. "I'm fine." She's had worse injuries on this boat.

She holds onto the beam tight as the boat rocks back and forth again. In the corner, there's a splash, water sloshing from Otto's tank—she's about to ask Evie what's happened, but Evie speaks first.

"He's okay," Evie calls out. "The octopus. He's just curled up in the corner, sleeping, I think." The boat roils again, and she hears Evie suck in a sharp breath.

"His name is Otto," she tells Evie, speaking as loud as she can over the hiss of the rain. "He's trapped here too."

"We need to get out of here," Evie replies. "All of us. There must be a way out."

Gripping the beam with one hand, the Girl stretches her leg out and feels for the bolt on her chain. "I was trying to get it free," she says. "There's a bolt loose, and I think the other one could be moved too, but it's too stiff."

Carefully, she moves closer to where Evie is bound and lifts the ankle to show her.

"You're right," Evie says, a hint of hope in her words. "If you wrapped it round the other beam, created some tension, then bounce it hard against the wood… It might only take a few hits."

"He'll hear us," the Girl says, swallowing the bile rising in her throat.

"No, he won't. This storm isn't going anywhere, he'll be distracted."

Maybe Evie is right—the sounds of the storm outside are loud, and the Curator's hearing has always been worse than hers. Maybe the rain will be enough to drown out everything else. It's all they can hope for.

As the storm quickens, adrenaline surges inside Evie and she watches the Girl manoeuvre the chain around the wooden beam. She twists it around, levering the edge of the bolt to the edge of the beam. Evie can tell from the Girl's face that she's in pain, wincing each time the metal moves against her skin. She struggles with it the first few times—she lifts and drops the shackle too gently and the bolt barely shifts.

"Twist it to the side, just a little," Evie instructs, and the Girl nods, moves into a better position. She tries again. One, two, three hits. Harder each time. Then another and the Girl cries out with the force of it.

"Keep going," Evie whispers, hoping she's right about the sound. Hoping the Curator won't come in and put a stop to them. She wonders once again how the Girl came to have barnacles for eyes. If the Curator didn't find her that way, did he do it to her himself? What does he plan to turn Evie into? They need to get free—she's not going to spend her life passed from one prison to another.

Come on, she urges the Girl as the waves surge so violently that something breaks beneath them—barrels she thinks, rolling back and forth.

Abruptly: a rattle and crack. Not from beneath, but from the Girl. The bolt slips out and the chains break loose.

They cry out triumphantly as the Girl stands, unsteady at first, still clutching the beam, her breath heavy.

Evie holds out her bound hands. "Three steps forward, slightly to your left, follow my voice," she says, and tentatively the Girl comes forward, careful step by careful step. And then she takes her hands, holds them so that they're standing across from one another, face to face.

"You're warm," the Girl says, holding Evie's hands as if it's the first time she's been touched in a long time. Evie realises it might be the same for her—the first time someone's held her out of warmth, not anger or hate.

"You did it."

The Girl lets out a bark of a laugh, then she's feeling around the rope for the knots the Curator made. "I need to free you too."

Evie tries to look at where the knot is, but it's too dark to see much, even with the Girl's shimmering form. But the Girl is already feeling along the edges of the rope, searching for the knot.

"Here," she whispers, and as she works away at it, more gently than the Curator, she hums her song and glows even brighter. In the corner, Evie notices Otto is moving in his tank—his limbs are stretched out across the whole front of the tank, as though he senses something has changed.

Evie feels like she's been holding her breath for minutes, when finally the rope loosens and the Girl unravels the binds.

"You did it!" she shouts, and she embraces the Girl, cherishes the warmth of it for a long moment even though the Girl's skin is stone cold.

"What next?" the Girl asks.

Evie puts her hand on the Girl's shoulder, cheeks flushed as she looks around. Then her gaze falls on the archway, remembering the hatch from earlier. "I think I've got an idea."

The Girl stands back in the shadows, pressed against the side of the archway as Evie instructed, waiting. The storm is settling now, the waves only a slow up and down. She listens to the sounds of the sea, listens to Otto in his tank, even to the sound of Evie's breathing in the corner where she's standing now, where the Curator left her. There's a certain calmness to the rhythm, of hearing her new companion and the sea, together almost as one.

A new sound echoes. Footsteps approach the main cabin door, then a click as it's unlocked. The Curator steps inside, heavy footed, his breath ragged and rasping.

"Where is she?" he shouts, and he's approaching Evie.

The Girl hopes he doesn't realise she's broken free from the ropes, that they wrapped them back loosely, hooking them into Evie's hands so she still appears bound. *An optical illusion*, she thinks.

"She's gone," Evie says, quiet. She might even be crying.

"What d'you mean, gone?"

A pause. "You left a bolt loose. She got free and headed through the archway. She must have escaped," Evie says. "*Please*, let me go," she adds, but the Curator doesn't respond. He marches towards the archway, and the Girl holds her breath. As he rounds the corner, Evie shouts: "Now!"

She rushes forwards, and with all her weight she hits the body of the Curator, shoving him. He stumbles, loses his footing, and slips into the hatch they opened earlier. He falls heavily. A snapping sound. A guttural cry. The Girl steps back. Evie is already at her side, and together they pull the hatch door over. They slip a whale vertebra into the handle to seal it tight. A moment of quiet passes, then there's a *thud thud* as the Curator yells, curses them. "I'll kill you!" he shouts. "Evil, vile girls. I'll kill you for this!"

"Do we just leave him there?" the Girl asks, and Evie squeezes her hand.

"Let's just go see where we are. We can figure it out. Together."

The Girl nods, liking the sound of together. "We need to help Otto first."

After scooping the poor octopus out—he seems to understand what's happening and wraps his limbs around her arm gently—the Girl follows Evie out to deck. There they stand, and she feels the sea breeze on her back, the cries of gulls around. The storm has settled, and all around her, the open sea calls.

She leans over the edge, putting her arm as close to the water as she can, and lets Otto slip into the sea. There's a splash, then another, as the octopus is finally back where he belongs. The Girl feels a pang in her chest. "Goodbye friend," she whispers, hoping she'll see him again, one way or another.

"He looks happy," Evie says with a laugh.

Then the Girl stands, listens for a moment. "It's too quiet."

"It's peaceful," Evie replies.

"No, I mean the—"

And then the voice booms from behind. "You idiot girls think you can trick and trap me on my own boat?"

They swivel around to face him, the Curator, wiping blood from his nose. He spits a mouthful of it onto the deck at his feet.

"There's more than one hatch. Now, I'll give you one chance to come back. I'll get better chains and rope, but spending some time below might be good for you first."

"We're not going anywhere with you," Evie says.

"Aye," he says. "So be it."

A rush of footsteps as the Curator careens towards them.

The Girl doesn't stop to think—she just grabs Evie around the waist and leaps into the water, after Otto. A splash, and a tangle of limbs, and the sharp cold of the sea.

And then, her barnacle eyes open.

The cold envelops Evie's body as she scrambles in the water, the Girl's arms tight around her waist. She screams out, tries to loosen the Girl's grip from around her, but she won't let go. And they're sinking deeper. In the haze of the water, she sees a form above, the heavy figure of the

Curator swimming around—except he looks strange. He has the head of an octopus.

Before she can make sense of it, the image fades. Lights dance in front of her eyes. Her lungs scream. She can't hold her breath much longer. She twists her body round as much as she can, to face the Girl. Her barnacle eyes are open, and within them there's a blackness, multiple eyes flickering and moving, wide and dark as an abyss. Then, it's like she's sinking into them.

The sea gives and the sea takes.

A voice in the Girl's head, old ancestral memories flooding into her mind. She was taken from her family, she remembers now, stolen by the Curator like she was nothing. She must return now, here where she belongs. Light unspools gradually, her vision returning with her memories. Dark shapes start to form, faint at first, and then they are glittering and bright, a myriad of colours and shapes and beauty all around. And she knows she must stay here, she must keep going down and down, beneath the sea.

Then, in front of her, a face. *Evie*, the girl who helped save her. She looks ethereal, her dark hair flowing behind her as they sink together. She starts to hum the tune that Evie liked, and tells her in the song, *We did it, we escaped, we returned to the sea. Now we can be together.* She smiles and holds her tighter.

Except, Evie isn't smiling. Her face is pale, eyes clasped shut, and there's a slow stream of bubbles escaping from her mouth.

Evie. She sings the word in her own tongue, the language she'd almost forgotten. *Wake up!* A siren cry. She shakes Evie, then she realises. She's disoriented, confused. This is her home, not Evie's.

She looks up to the bright surface, and swims as fast as she can.

A tightness in her chest. The cold sea all around her.

"Evie. Wake up. Evie, breathe. *Please*, please wake up." The voice echoes, melodic, familiar.

Evie opens her eyes slowly and rasps out a breath. The water burns her throat as she coughs it from her lungs. She blinks the stinging salt from her eyes and looks at the Girl before her.

The Girl with barnacles for eyes, transformed, eyes blinking rapidly, skin shimmering grey, belonging as much to the sea as any other creature she's seen. She is holding Evie so gently, cradling her within the calming waves as they float together under sunlight that is just starting to break through from the grey skies above.

The Girl lifts her hands to Evie's head, to brush the hair from her cheeks, and Evie notices they're webbed, her nails sharpened into claws.

Can't monsters be beautiful?

"I saw a man with an octopus for his head," she says, as though waking from a dream.

The Girl smiles, her teeth sharper than before. "Otto," she says. "And the Curator. He's gone now."

As though in response, Otto swims up to Evie and squeezes her arm, gently, climbing up to her shoulder. She can't help but smile, the brightness of the octopus returning.

"I'm sorry," the Girl says. "I got lost for a moment, I wasn't myself, I never meant to…"

"It's okay," Evie says softly, and she looks behind her, the boat bobbing up and down with the waves, not too far from where they are. "We're free now."

The Girl nods. "I remember my name," she says. "Maira."

"Maira," Evie whispers, enjoying how the word sounds on her lips. "You're home."

Maira smiles. "I think I've seen this before," she says, tilting her chin towards the Curator's boat. "You, captaining the boat, and me, swimming at its side."

Evie warms at the thought. "I like that image."

"Where shall we go?"

"Wherever we wish," Maira says. "As long as we can stay together."

"We and the sea," Evie amends.

Maira pushes off through the water, pulling Evie alongside her, effortless, graceful, and Otto follows along beside them.

For the first time in what feels like forever, Evie takes a breath that she's not afraid might be stolen from her.

THE BALLAD OF HORSE GIRL

Bitter Karella

1. The Church of the Last Redoubt

The canyon was choked with prickly pears, growing in vast tangled mats that climbed the sheer cliff faces and left only a narrow passage along the throat of the gully through which the Horse Girl now traveled. The Horse Girl moved slowly because she wanted to avoid the thorns, but, when she was out of sight of men and wished to move quickly, she could drop to her hands and the tips of her toes and gallop with great speed as was the way of her people. She wore a Stetson hat and a poncho of Navajo design to protect her from the blazing sun and to fit in among the white men, but, if she had her druthers, she would not bother with such ornamentation. Her feet were bare and so thickly caked with callouses that they more resembled hooves, and her gnarled knuckles were similarly enveloped. Slung over her back with leather straps, she carried a pinewood casket, too small for her own use unless she folded up her arms and legs just so.

"Almost there, Lil' Varmint," she said. "Y'all hold tight in there."

Something inside the casket knocked two sharp little raps in response.

The Horse Girl moved mostly during the early hours of the morning and the late hours of the evening, when long shadows provided some momentary relief from the sweltering desert sun. She slept in crevasses among the rocks during the day, when it was too hot to travel, and at night, when the waning moon didn't give enough light to pick her way through the thorn yards.

The prickly pears watched her pass, silent sentinels under the shimmering red sun.

The prickly pears were unique here, growing in tortured spiral formations that superstitious folks could easily interpret as too human. The Horse Girl was not superstitious, but even she could see how the cacti stretched out their thorny pads like grasping hands, and how the holes bored by gilded flickers or Gila woodpeckers resembled empty eye sockets and gaping maws. The cacti hadn't always been there, people said; only a few short years ago the canyon had been barren. Up until the missionaries found it easier to convert the local natives into corpses rather than Christians. After that, the prickly pears began to thrive, and folks claimed they grew wherever native blood spilled on the ground and they didn't stop growing because there was a lot of native blood spilled on the ground. White men feared to go into the canyon at night because, and the Horse Girl knew this well, white men were extremely scared of ghosts. Probably because ghosts had reason to dislike the white men.

But if indeed the cacti held some malevolent power, they chose not to molest the Horse Girl as she passed through their midst. The ghosts, if there were ghosts, remained asleep in their spiny cocoons and the Horse Girl passed quietly between them. Eventually, the Horse Girl's ankle fell upon a tripwire hidden in the dust and a series of copper keys and battered coffee pots raised a jangling cacophony—the first sounds to disturb the stillness of the canyon in all her days of travel. The Horse Girl frowned, a bead of sweat dripping down her forehead and cutting a path through the grime.

"So much for the element of surprise," she muttered, and whatever rode with her in the casket knocked once to indicate agreement.

Stealth was the Horse Girl's main advantage and now that was blown. Oh well. Too late to go back. Her quarry would know she was coming; she just had to hope for the best. She pressed onward.

It wasn't long after that she started to hear music on the breeze, the angelic voices of a church choir. At the apex of the canyon stood a little white-washed church with a leaning bell tower. It was slowly collapsing in on itself, the door and windows nailed over with boards. The music came from inside. Whatever congregation met there, they had been meeting for a long time.

An intricate mandala pattern was scratched into the ground surrounding the church. The Horse Girl could not be certain of the symbols' meaning, but the cacti refused to cross the pattern, so the Horse Girl assumed it must be some form of protective sigil. She was not to be deterred, however. She rolled her shoulders and let the casket fall to the ground, then, leaving it where it fell, she stepped over the edge of the pattern and marched toward the church.

"Sit tight, Lil' Varmint; I'll be back."

Inside, the congregation was still singing. That was good. Maybe the tripwire hadn't alerted them after all. Typical Christians. Always too busy with their songs to notice anything out in the real world.

The Horse Girl heaved her shoulder against the rotting door once, twice, and on the third attempt she felt the flimsy boards buckle—only slightly but just enough to give her hope. She threw her full weight at the door again. It collapsed inward and the Horse Girl tumbled into the church riding along a cloud of dust.

She stumbled to her feet, hand hovering over her pistol. The nave was a large, white-washed chamber, two rows of wooden pews flanking a central aisle marked by a threadbare red carpet. The pews were filled with parishioners, who ignored the Horse Girl's noisy entry. The Horse Girl looked from one parishioner to another. They weren't real. The pews were filled with scarecrows, ratty clothes stuffed with hay, crude faces scrawled across stuffed burlap sacks or carved into rotting pumpkins. The ghostly choir continued to sing its hymn, though the scarecrows did not move. The sounds of organ music filled the church, though the dilapidated organ in the corner stood silent and unmanned, mice nesting in its pipes.

The Horse Girl nickered in confusion and stamped her foot nervously. But this was not the time to lose heart.

"Parson?" she called out. There was no response, save her own voice echoing back. But she knew he must be here. He wouldn't leave the protection of his sigils, she knew, not while ghosts and possibly worse things lurked outside.

She drew her six-shooter and cautiously tiptoed down the aisle, stealing glances left and right. She was in uncharted territory. No, she was not a superstitious person at all, but she still couldn't shake the awful conviction that at any moment those scarecrows might just rise as one and fly at her. It was only as she approached the front of the church and discovered the source of the singing that she relaxed. A wax cylinder spun on a phonograph carefully balanced on the rim of the pulpit.

She saw a small door set into the wall behind the altar. Her quarry, she reasoned, must be within.

The Horse Girl grabbed the handle and turned. It was not locked. The door swung open silently and she aimed her pistol into the darkened vestry.

"Padre?" said the Horse Girl.

A gold leaf bible flew from the dark and hit the Horse Girl square in the face. She lurched backwards and discharged her gun impotently into the air. A black shape burst from the vestry like a bat out of hell, and sailed down the aisle, knocking scarecrows from their pews.

"Hold it right there!" shouted the Horse Girl. She aimed her pistol but hesitated. She could not risk killing her quarry. Not yet.

The black shape reached the broken doorway, where it paused, as if suddenly afraid to cross the threshold to leave the church. Now the Horse Girl could see it clearly. It was a young man, wearing a black cassock and wide-brimmed hat.

"Hang on there, parson, I ain't about to do ya no harm," said the Horse Girl. "I just wanna talk."

The parson shrieked again and ran along the wall, until he reached the twisting stairwell that led up to the belfry.

The Horse Girl could hear his feet slapping against the wooden stair slats as he ascended, two at a time in his panic. The Horse Girl followed, running round and round and round, up and up, until she burst forth into the daylight and felt the dry wind on her face. The belfry was open to the elements and she could see the ground so many, many feet below. A dizzying height.

The parson stood at the edge of the platform, cowering behind the big iron bell. His black robes whipped in the wind.

"Demon!" cried the parson in a trembling voice. He pointed a quivering finger at the Horse Girl. "Go back to the hell that spawned you!"

"Easy there, padre," said the Horse Girl, who could see from the situation that she was going to need a light touch. "I ain't no demon. I'm as flesh and blood as you. Don't do anything rash."

"Foul spirit! Get back! I know what you are! I name thee—tempter! Satan! Lucifer!"

"Let's calm down now, padre," said the Horse Girl. She held up empty hands before her to show her good intentions. "I'm not gonna hurt you. I just need some help."

"Liar! I know what you want! Don't think I don't know the tricks of heathens! Even from beyond the grave, they send their ghouls to torment me! Who made you? The Pomo? The Chumash? The Yokuts?"

The Horse Girl was not originally of Alta California. Her people—and when she thought of her people, she didn't think of the woman who birthed her or the man who sired her, those people who had been murdered when she was too young to remember; she thought of the people who had adopted her, the wild mustangs of the Plains, the pintos and palominos who taught her to gallop the lonesome prairie and graze the sage grass, who taught her to whicker and whinny and speak the many tongues of horse—her people came from the great steppes of Nebraska and Iowa. But the parson saw her dark skin and her black hair and believed she was of Indian stock.

"I don't know what you done to the Pomo or the Chumash or the Yokuts," said the Horse Girl, "but they ain't sent me. I came of my own accord."

"I never harmed any Christian!" howled the parson, as if he hadn't heard a word the Horse Girl said. "Everything I've done, I've done for the glory of the good Lord! That's why He gifted me this sanctuary! He protects me here!" He laughed mirthlessly. "I can hear them all, wailing and whining for revenge… But they cannot harm me in this holy place! *You* cannot harm me in this holy place, fiend!"

"I ain't gonna harm ya, padre," she repeated. "I just wanna take you out for a drink."

"Stay back, harlot! You shall not tempt me!"

"I've had enough of this." She ran at the parson and smashed into him, propelling the both of them over the edge of the bell tower. His hat flew off and his thick black hair fluttered in the wind. For a moment, they hung suspended in the air as if buoyed by the sheer force of the parson's surprise. And then they fell, crashing through the shingled canopy over the front door below and hitting the boardwalk in a shower of wooden shards and with the force of a comet making impact. And that's where they lay.

2. The Cantina at the Crossroads

The Cantina at the Crossroads had two resident cats. One was an old black moggy with a regal bearing and fur as sleek as satin, who would graciously accept pets for a finite amount of time before wandering off to some secluded side room where she could curl up and be lulled to sleep by the sounds of laughter and merriment. The other was a young tom, mackerel tabby in coloration, who could not drink his fill of attention, who demanded to climb on tables and perch in laps and was not above slapping a cowpoke's hand with his paw to suggest that the cowpoke would be better off using that hand to pet him than in whatever other activity it might have been presently engaged. It was this tabby who now suddenly leaped onto the table between the Horse Girl and the parson—causing the latter to recoil in surprise—and chirped loudly for attention.

"You play cards, parson?" asked the Horse Girl, as she shuffled a deck of cards between her fingers. She flipped one onto the table; it revealed a simple gray edifice against a black background, a jagged yellow bolt of lightning striking its spire.

The Horse Girl sucked air between her teeth and shook her head. "Bad luck, parson, bad luck!"

The parson did not respond. His eyes darted to and fro, and it seemed that the sounds of music and laughter from the other rooms did little to assuage his nerves. She looked at him. The parson had the soft eyes and unlined face of a man who had never had to think very long or very deeply about any subject. No doubt, he was one of those lucky men whom the Lord had called early. She imagined that the Lord took his hand when he was still a boy and led him to the seminary and then to the pulpit and, finally, when he grew tired of the easy life in the east and heard rumors that there were heathens and savages out west that needed to hear the good word, out to Alta California. He was the sort of man that would do well there, who could attract the ladyfolk to his church to hear his sermons simply on the strength of his innocent good looks. He was handsome, youthful with a beautiful crown of jet-black hair but just a dignified hint of premature grey at his temples, and possessed luscious full lips that would make every word out of his mouth ring with an extra vibration of truth.

"I expect you're not a gambler, being a man of the cloth and all," said the Horse Girl, shuffling the remainder of the deck. "I ain't never had much luck at cards myself and I expect it's for the best, seein' as ya wouldn't wanna get too overly fond of 'em."

The parson remained silent. The tabby stared at the cards in wide-eyed confusion. Several clocks struck the hour. Every inch of wall space in the Cantina at the Crossroads was filled with ornate cuckoo clocks, each one set to a different time, their constant ticking and chiming barely audible over the tinny jangle of the pianola and the laughter and chatter of people. Elsewhere in the building, roughnecks were throwing back whiskey at the bar and desperados were huddled into little clots playing poker and dice in secluded alcoves. The air was thick with a miasma of pipe tobacco and cooking grease and the smell of sizzling bacon and bubbling stew. The Cantina at the Crossroads was dark and smoky and loud, but there was a delicious, warm feeling of welcome; a visit here felt like coming home after a long day of work.

"Where are we?" said the parson suddenly.

The Horse Girl ignored him. "Now this tower," she said, tapping a finger against the face of the revealed card,

"I reckon that's your little church, where you was all holed up. And I reckon this here lightning? That's me bustin' you outta yer hidey hole."

"Where are we?" repeated the parson with growing agitation. The tabby cat, who did not like being ignored, meowed loudly.

"You've made yourself a lot of enemies," said the Horse Girl, now reaching out and stroking the tabby cat so that he arched his back and vibrated his tail. "A surprising number of enemies for someone in your line of work, I'd reckon. I can see why you'd hide yourself away from the world in your little church like that."

Now the parson nervously wrung his hands together, his eyes darting about. "Where did you bring me? Where is this?!"

"A man in your situation would do well to hire protection. And it's just your luck that I happen to be in the protection business myself. I'd offer a demonstration, but I feel like our little rumble at your church has already showed what I can do."

The tabby waddled over toward the parson and rubbed his face against the parson's knuckle. The parson was ill at ease but not so ill at ease that he could ignore the exhortation; he raised his hand and rubbed the cat's ear between his thumb and forefinger. The cat vibrated with pleasure.

"Best of all, I'm willing to waive my usual fee. I'm offering you my protection gratis, at least for the duration of our association. You can't beat that deal, parson."

"I never did nothing wrong," said the parson. "I never hurt anybody."

"No? Then why are you so scared?"

The parson gulped. It sounded like a toilet plunger. "I never hurt a Christian soul," he said, amending his earlier statement. "You can't hold me responsible for the fate of heathens! They're not supposed to come back!"

"Seems like some of them heathens had souls too, though, padre. Guess you didn't figure on that. And now them heathens sure are spittin' mad. They ain't too keen on you. So, again, I'm gonna lay out your choices. You can stick with me and avail yourself of that aforementioned protection. Or, if you prefer, you can go back to your church. I'm a reasonable gal, ain't gonna hold you here against your will."

The Horse Girl leaned forward across the table, resting her weight on her elbows, and lowered her voice.

"But it's a long walk back to your church, padre. A real long walk. I reckon word's getting out that you ain't safe in your little hidey hole behind your sigils and your crosses no more. I reckon some of your old friends might be aimin' to meet up with ya along the way for a, heh, friendly bit of conversation."

"Why did you bring me here?! What do you want with me?!"

"Nothin' big. See, I got a present I aim to deliver to an old friend and I figure you're gonna help me out, seein' as you know him. The Hangin' Judge."

The parson visibly shivered. When he spoke, his voice quavered.

"The Hangin' Judge? You're insane. You can't fight the Hangin' Judge."

"I can. And I will. There's a bounty."

"You won't ever collect it. I know that much for sure."

"You seem awful sure of that, parson. What do you know about the Hangin' Judge?"

The parson fidgeted, nervously wringing his hands. "I know he can't be killed by any man born of woman. That's why they call him the Hangin' Judge. They hanged him twice—twice!—and he wouldn't stay dead. They say he sold his soul to the devil to live forever."

"Everyone knows that about the Hangin' Judge. Tell me something new."

"Nobody knows where he came from. There's some that say he got his start back east, part of the Tammany Hall machine in New York City, but I've never known anyone there that remembers him. The earliest I heard of the Hangin' Judge he just appeared, outta nowhere, crossing the Plains, making his fortune in scalp bounties and horse paste, 'til he got wind that they'd struck snake oil in Alta California. Next thing, he shows up in Santa Diablo, buying votes 'til he controls the whole of the territory north of Monterey, up where the Californios don't have any garrisons. And he's been expanding his influence ever since."

"He still in Santa Diablo?"

"That's the word. What's this got to do with me? I'm just a simple man of God, I've got no business with the Hangin' Judge! I've never crossed him!"

The Horse Girl shuffled the deck of cards a second time and flipped a second card.

"Eight of Cups," said the Horse Girl. "Reckon that means our association ain't gonna last too long, padre. Hard times ahead. Real hard times. But I mean to bring the Hangin' Judge in by hook or by crook, and you've got a part to play in this charade, padre, even if you don't know it yet."

"It's a fool's errand," said the parson. "He can't be killed!"

"You seem real sure of that, padre. I reckon you know more about that than you're letting on. How you know that?"

The parson looked defeated. "I… I brokered the deal."

"That's some nasty business for a man of God."

The parson exploded: "He tricked me! I thought the Hangin' Judge was a good man! When I came to Alta California, he was the one who donated the land for the church! He gave the money to build the church! And he was there, every Sunday! I thought he was a godly man!"

"So you helped him sell his soul to the devil?"

"Every parson knows how to conjure the devil. The instructions are right there, in the Bible, only you're not supposed to follow them. That's the whole point of having them in there, to resist the temptation. But the Hangin' Judge, he said that the good would outweigh the bad. If he could just talk to the devil, he could negotiate for...so much. So much good for Alta California, so much good for the church! I thought I was doing the right thing!"

"So he can't be killed by any man born of woman," said the Horse Girl. "See, that's the rub right there, eh?"

The parson sat up straight, his eyes flashing with a new resolve. "I know what you're thinking. Do not be so foolish, Horse Girl, to think the Hangin' Judge can be brought down on a mere technicality."

"I would never be so foolish," said the Horse Girl. She kicked at the small casket, which was under the table. Something within knocked back and rustled inside. "I got a plan."

"Who's offering this bounty?" said the parson, suspicious. "Who would offer a bounty on a man that can't die?"

He looked away toward the sound of the door creaking open where a tall thin woman in black emerged from behind the Horse Girl. Her own jet-black hair was tied back into a severe bun under a towering jeweled peineta, and her face was painted in whorls of red and white with black rings around her yellow eyes. The parson took a single look at her and jumped from his seat, shrieking as he scuttled backwards until his back hit the wall. The tabby cat flew across the room at the sudden noise, dodging between the woman's feet and disappearing into the labyrinth of rooms beyond with an agitated yowl.

"La Muerte! Have mercy! For the love of God, have mercy! You brought me to her!"

"Sit down and shut up, parson," said the Horse Girl. "That's just your guilty conscious talking. Now sit your ass down before you offend our lovely hostess." She turned to the woman. "Coffin varnish for me. And another shot for my friend here."

"How can I drink when La Muerte is here to take me away!?" howled the parson.

The Horse Girl nodded. "Good for you. A real nasty habit, gets you in all sorts of scrapes." To the woman, she rephrased: "Coffin varnish for me. And a nice frosty glass of sarsaparilla for my friend. We been smelling that stew you got bubbling since we got here and it's making me mighty hungry. Don't suppose I could trouble you for a couple bowls? It's just the thing we need to keep up our strength for the journey ahead."

The woman peered down her nose at the Horse Girl with an air of haughty disdain. Finally, she said, "There is no journey ahead for you, señorita. The Cantina at the Crossroads is where your journey ends."

"I don't reckon that's so. Believe me, I didn't want to come! But I knew I could impose upon your hospitality just one last time… One last time before I bring the Judge in?"

"You have been promising to bring me the Judge for a long time. And yet, I do not see him here. All I see is this scarecrow." She tilted her jaw toward the parson and sniffed derisively. "What do you want me to do with him?"

The Horse Girl put a hand on the woman's hip, touching the material of her dress between thumb and forefinger in a subtle gesture, as if she was merely curious about the fabric, but that gentlest touch said so much more. "I was hoping I wouldn't have to leave the scarecrow here. I was hoping you'd give us both safe passage."

"*Both of you?* It is bad enough that you ask for yourself! You are unbelievable!"

"Listen, I told ya I got a plan. I got a plan that's gonna bring the Hangin' Judge down, but it's complicated. It's got moving parts. And the parson here, he's a vital component of it all. So ya gotta think about the long haul, the big prize.

You give us safe passage and I guarantee, the next time ya see me I'm gonna have the Hangin' Judge for ya. I guarantee it."

"You have a silver tongue, Horse Girl. You have given me guarantees before. I told you last time, do not come back without the Judge. I told you what would happen if you did."

"I reckon you're right, I done broke my word and come back too soon. So I reckon there ain't much for me to do, except throw myself on the mercy of the court. I guess the big question is, how much do you want the Judge? Ya know, if'n you let me and the parson go, we'll be back eventually. Ain't nothing gonna deny you your due in the end. But the Judge? Well, the only way you'll ever get him is if I bring him here. So I guess ya gotta ask yourself how much do ya really want him? You know I'm the only one to do it. The Judge, he's in tight with the powers that be. The good Lord above clearly ain't got no problem with him livin' forever and the devil below don't care neither. And ain't no earthly power but me gonna intervene. I'm the last one. Hell, I'd do it even if there weren't no bounty."

The Horse Girl tapped her fingers rhythmically against the table top and her eyes looked into the distance of memory. After a pause, she continued, but quieter.

"The Judge killed them all. All the horses of the Plains, the great herds of Nebraska and Iowa. I saw him do it, saw him put them all through his machine. I swore I'd make him pay. I swore to God, swore to the devil, swore to anyone listening, I'd make him pay and I wouldn't shuffle off this mortal coil 'til I done it. Please. Send me back. I swore it. Don't make me a liar."

The woman didn't answer, but pressed her lips together into a thin line of rage. Then she relented and said, "This time—this *last* time—I will grant you safe passage. But if I see you again, Horse Girl, whether you have the Judge or not, it will be our last meeting. Do you understand?"

"I understand. And when ya say safe passage, ya do mean my friend here's included in that too, right?"

The woman looked at the parson, who was still pressed against the far wall, shaking with terror.

"You say he is important to your plan?"

The casket under the table rattled as if it intended to move. The Horse Girl grabbed it with both hands and hoisted it into her lap, wrapping her arms around it to secure it. "Can't bring ya the Hangin' Judge without him."

"Fine. Then I shall grant him safe passage as well. But mark my words, Horse Girl, this is your last chance. I look forward to our next meeting."

"Can't say that I feel the same way," muttered the Horse Girl under her breath as the woman swept out of the room. But out loud, she said, "Hey, how about that stew?"

"Good Lord in Heaven!" said the parson in the corner. "What is this place? What manner of devilry is this?"

"Sit down and stop embarrassing me," said the Horse Girl. "A man of God such as yourself should be familiar with shit like this. Don't they teach ya anything in seminary? A man's gotta meet his maker eventually. I should think you'd be champin' at the bit."

Moments later, the woman returned with two bowls of thick stew full of meat and potatoes. She placed them on the table and silently swept out of the room again.

"Much obliged, ma'am," said the Horse Girl to her retreating backside. She grabbed her spoon and scooped a chunk of potato into her mouth. "That's why I ain't ever got into religion. If a parson can't face the end with joy in his heart, what chance is there for the rest of us poor sinners? Now parson, eat up. We got a ways to go and we ain't gonna find no place more hospitable between here and Santa Diablo."

3. Under the Mountain

Sugar & Sache squeezed her eyes closed and silently prayed that her gorge would stay down as the elevator descended the mine shaft at a dizzying pace. Her hands gripped the guardrail so tightly that her knuckles blanched, and she kept every muscle in her body rigid for fear that, were she to relax, even for a moment, she would fly into pieces.

Sugar & Sache was a beautiful calico woman, her whole body—which her husband the Judge had explored many times—awash in colors, but in her modest dress the only evidence of her pigmentation was that the left side of her face was milky white and the right side was mottled brown with just a dab of orange between her eyebrows.

The other occupants of the elevator did not experience the same vertigo or, if they did, they masked their discomfort well. The Judge was here, of course, and chief among them. The rest, other than Sugar & Sache, were the Judge's posse, shifty characters he had picked up along the way on his journey to power. Shifty characters often found a friendship with the Judge to be very useful, seeing as they frequently found themselves in a tight spot with the law, and the Judge in turn found it useful to have a certain stable of shifty characters to draw upon for odd jobs. There was Two-Eyed Mulligan, whose entire body other than the top of his head was covered in red curly hair; Skunkface Sally, whose face was naturally coal black and grease-painty; Angelhair Horchata, who was trained in the twin arts of seduction and assassination; and the Jackelope, renowned for his speed and his filed teeth. And then there were the McCready twins, who followed only their own rules in all things.

The elevator hit bottom with a hiss of hydraulics, and Sugar & Sache's stomach descended from its perch in her chest a moment later. She sighed in relief, releasing her death grip on the metal bars and following her husband as he stepped down from the elevator platform. The Judge had to duck his head under the crossbeam to enter the mine slope. He did not wait for her and soon disappeared into the darkness.

"Husband!" she cried. "Husband, please wait!"

"Follow my voice, wife. There's light ahead. Do you see it?"

She felt her way along the tunnel, bumbling after him, her hands pressing against the walls. It was natural stone, supported by wooden arches and, further down the shaft, she could see the welcome flickers of wick lamps briefly eclipsed by her husband's giant shadow. The stone was wet and greasy, dripping with pure liquid snake oil, which congealed into shallow puddles along the corridor and finally into a deeper pool that filled the cavern into which they emerged. Hand-painted warning signs hung at intervals: DANGER!! BLASTING AREA!!! and KEEP OUT!!

Behind them, the posse entered the cave.

Up ahead, in the distant dimness of the cavern, Sugar & Sache knew there was a man because she could hear the steady KLONK KLONK KLONK of his pick axe hitting the wall. The snake oil lake glimmered in the sputtering light, rainbow ribbons of brilliance rippling along its surface. She could sense the change in the Judge as his eyes fell upon that prize—the subtle quickening of breath and pulse that signaled his rising excitement, the greedy glint in his eye. The Judge intended to have it, consequences be damned, and it was that single-minded ambition that had made him richest man in all of Alta California and the biggest snake oil baron west of the Mississippi. This small pool could be worth hundreds, possibly even thousands of dollars. Concentrated, purified, and bottled, it was a potent remedy for scabies, scurvy, cholera, Welshman's despair, even the intangible squirms. The scientists said that it was made from the decomposed remains of ancient snakes, while the holy men said it was a trick of the devil, placed underground to deceive people into believing that snakes had once existed. But what was undeniable was that the entire patent medicine business—and, by extension, the American economy—depended on a steady influx of the stuff. Whoever controlled the snake oil mines would control the country.

The fortune a man could make in snake oil dwarfed any fortune a man could make in horse paste.

The Judge waved for them to follow him as he edged along the shoreline of the snake oil lake, following the KLONK KLONK KLONK until its source came into view. It was a short, white-haired man with a bushy white beard, his checkered flannel shirt soaked with sweat. The little man was nestled inside a clockwork exoskeleton, pulling at levers that controlled the enormous pick axe arms now clawing at the cave walls—KLONK KLONK

KLONK—the exoskeleton's massive metal struts elevating him above the cavern-filling pool of shimmering snake oil.

"Mr. Bunions?" called the Judge. "Gabby Bunions?"

"Don't like no visitors," shouted the man without turning to face them. "I told ya that last time, ya dang buzzard!"

Gabby pulled some mechanism inside the exoskeleton and it turned, hydraulics hissing and clanking, to face the group. It raised its pick axe arms menacingly. Several members of the posse reached for their six-shooters out of habit, but the Judge raised his hand for them to relax.

"You like it?" said Gabby, slapping the console in front of him. "I done made it myself! Gabby ain't no greenhorn when it comes ta tinkerin'! Now git offa mah claim, ya no-good galoots!" He caught sight of Sugar & Sache among their number and he tipped his hat apologetically. "Beggin' yer pardon, ma'am."

The Judge took a step backwards. "I came because I thought we could reach an agreement, Gabby. It would be in your best interest."

"Dagnabbit! Ain't nobody gonna move me offa my property! I done worked this claim fair and square!"

The Judge adjusted his bolo tie casually. "Mr. Bunions—Gabby. You've really done well for yourself here, but you're only one man. One man can only do so much. The Dives Mining Consortium is prepared to make a very generous offer for your claim."

Sugar & Sache saw that the Judge did not carry with him a satchel or bag, nothing that could possibly contain the cash or legal documents he claimed ready to transfer to Gabby. That meant the Judge was confident Gabby would not sell. And even if Gabby did by some freak of fate agree to sell, the Judge did not intend to pay.

"Ya don't scare me, Judge!" yelled Gabby. "Yer days are numbered! Ya know what they say—the Horse Girl is on the move! She's comin', Judge, an' she'll put a stop to ya!"

The Judge tensed. Sugar & Sache could feel it, could tell by a sudden change in the air, could feel the Judge's entire massive body seize up. A vein pulsed in his enormous sequoia neck and he balled his ham-sized hands into fists.

"Who told you that?" he said quietly.

"Everyone's sayin' it!" shouted Gabby. He pulled a lever and the mech jabbed a pick axe skyward in a gesture that was probably supposed to be obscene. "They say she's crossin' the Boneyard now and she'll be in Santa Diablo soon! Best say your prayers, Judge! She ain't gonna let a no-good yellow-bellied galoot like you keep pushing us around!"

"The Horse Girl," said the Judge slowly and deliberately, "is a myth. I killed her and all of her kind, long ago, when I cleared the prairies. She will not save you, Gabby. She is not coming. The only thing that will save you, that *can* save you, is you—if you agree to sell your claim. This is your last chance."

"Get the hell offa my property!" shouted Gabby. The exoskeleton waded into the snake oil lake, toward the Judge and his posse, waving its pick axes in a threat.

Sugar & Sache didn't have the gift of prophecy. She didn't need any kind of foresight to see the future, exactly as it would happen, laid out before her as clear as a diamond in her mind's eye. She could see the shimmering surface of the snake oil lake, resplendent in its rainbow sheen, on fire—a blazing inferno, hotter than hell—and she could see Gabby's charred, mangled corpse floating right there in the middle of it. The Judge held the deed to every snake oil claim north of the Boneyard and he would not rest until he held every claim in Alta California. Gabby Bunions thought he would be the lone hold-out because, like so many old-timers, he thought that you could defeat a bully like Judge Lazarus Dives by standing your ground. But it took more than a few gruff words to make the Hangin' Judge turn tail. The Hangin' Judge had all the power of the law at his back and only naïve old-timers like Gabby ever thought that would be used for good.

Sugar & Sache grabbed the Judge's sleeve, a sudden wave of sentimental pity washing over her. "Oh! Oh! Husband, please! Couldn't you leave him his claim? Just this once? He's just a poor old man. He doesn't have anything else."

The Judge chuckled deep in his chest and placed a massive hand on her slender shoulder. His weight upon her grew heavier and heavier until she was certain he would break her.

"My wife," rumbled the Judge, nodding to the posse. "Such a soft-hearted creature! But isn't it within the nature of womenfolk to be tender? Ain't that what we love about them?"

The Judge's posse politely murmured their agreement. Sugar & Sache blushed, unable to speak.

"She's got such a delicate constitution. Let's go, boys. Let's not give this old-timer any trouble."

He looked to his posse and what he communicated to them with that look was lost in the shadows so that Sugar & Sache didn't see. But she could guess.

"Y'all best run!" shouted Gabby, waving the exoskeleton's drill arms. He had stopped advancing toward them, apparently confident that they were leaving.

The Judge steered her back toward the elevator. She peered over her shoulder and saw the Judge's posse was not following.

"Your posse!" she said. "They're…they're not coming?"

"They'll catch up," said the Judge. "They just gotta work out some logistics with that old-timer. They'll catch up in a minute."

Sugar & Sache knew she shouldn't say anything more. She knew she should just quietly leave with the Judge. But she couldn't help herself. She stopped in her tracks, so suddenly that the Judge almost tripped over her tiny form, and turned back toward Gabby.

"Mr. Bunions! Is it true—is the Horse Girl coming?"

Sugar & Sache could feel the Judge's silent rage, so thick it was like a physical being in the room with them. It was like a caged animal, furious and feral, and she knew it would be uncaged when they were alone...

Gabby raised a pick axe arm in a salute. The old-timer seemed to have a soft spot for a refined lady. "You best believe it, little lady! The Horse Girl, she's a-comin'! And when she gets here...she'll set us all free, you mark my words!"

"Let's go," said the Judge, his enormous hand squeezing her shoulder until she thought he would break it off.

"You better run, ya varmint!" yelled Gabby's voice as they hustled up the corridor toward the elevator. "The Horse Girl's gonna cut ya down! Ain't no runnin' from the Horse Girl! Ya can't outrun hell!"

Sugar & Sache did not dare say another word now. She was quiet as she rode the elevator back up the shaft, the Judge at her side. She was quiet as they boarded the stagecoach and started back for Santa Diablo. She was quiet as they rode away, watching through the window as the world passed by. And she was quiet when, as they were a sufficient distance away from the mountain, she heard a thunderous explosion and spied a gout of flame shooting from the distant mine shaft where only a few minutes ago she had ascended. She was not surprised, although she had tried to tell herself that she was.

"Oh no," said the Judge in a bored voice. "Hope no one was hurt."

Sugar & Sache didn't respond.

"You best put any thoughts about the Horse Girl out of your mind, wife," said the Judge. "That old-timer's off his rocker. There ain't no Horse Girl no more. You know I put a stop to her."

"Yes, husband."

"And don't get to thinking she's coming to save you. If they let her outta hell, she's only comin' to kill. She'll be coming to kill you as sure as she's coming to kill me."

Sugar & Sache closed her eyes, but she could still see the flames. She could see the flames all the way back to Santa Diablo.

4. *Encounter in the Boneyard*

"There's someone following us," said the parson in his typical whine.

The Boneyard occupied a section of otherwise useless desert between Corpus Collosum on the Alkaline Flats basin and Puerto Nalgas on the Baja coastline, an endless expanse of wooden crosses flanking a dirt road to nowhere. They were mostly soldiers, buried where they fell during the Battle of Buena Verde when a ragtag coalition of American volunteers under Sgt. Hubert Bugbear succumbed to the might of the Mexican army under General Maria Teresa García Ramírez de Arroyo. Folks generally traveled this area by tumbleweed or stagecoach, so that they could complete the journey before the sun dipped and the shadows grew long. But again, the Horse Girl didn't care much for superstitions and the ghosts of white men scared her about as much as the ghosts of Indians, meaning not at all. However, this was bandit country, and bandits were men of flesh and blood, and men of flesh and blood did concern the Horse Girl. She walked quickly, not galloping, just walking at a brisk but steady pace as a courtesy to the parson who did not share her stamina and who was forced to stumble along behind her, led by a rope bound around his wrists.

The Horse Girl squinted at the horizon, where there churned a cloud of dust so vast it was as if a whole posse was riding out to meet them. She peered through her field glasses to check again. Now she could see the dust wasn't dust at all, but a dense white mist slowly rolling over the plain. Tiny blue lights, like cold fireflies, bobbed and weaved in the fog.

"Shit," said the Horse Girl. She yanked on the rope and her unwilling companion stumbled closer to her. "You done made a lot of enemies, parson, and I reckon word got out that you're here."

"We shouldn't have come this way! Good Lord preserve us!" The parson shrieked and fell to his knees. He pulled his book from his cassock, placed it on the ground, and flipped it open to a familiar page before he started mumbling and muttering under his breath in a quavery, panicked voice.

The Horse Girl watched this scene unfold passively before asking, "What are you doing?"

The parson didn't look up. "Praying for salvation. Something you wouldn't know about!"

"Is that how you do it?"

Now the parson looked up. "Scoff if you want, apostate! I'd recommend you get down on your knees too—if you want the good Lord to save you!"

"Aw, he ain't listenin'."

Not too far away, there was a twisty red manzanita tree growing up out of the dirt. The Horse Girl walked over to it and broke off a branch. She swished it through the air, once, twice, three times, as if testing it out, then walked back toward the parson and, very quickly and roughly, touched its tip to the dirt and drew a circle around the two of them. Then she waited as the parson continued to pray.

The fog rolled across the plain too quickly for fog, eating the tombstones as it advanced. When it reached them, it parted as it touched the circle as if it had hit a wall. Yet the blue lights still weaved here and there. The fog bank spilled around the circle, thick as pea soup, until they were surrounded. But it did not breach the circle.

The parson continued to pray, louder, more fervently.

"Haku! 'Asku pi?" said the Horse Girl in Ventureño. There was no response, so she tried again, this time in

Yawelmani: "Wat-uk-ma?" Finally, she said in English: "Who are you?"

This elicited a response.

"How dee do, parson!" said a high-pitched voice. And then a lower voice responded with the same: "How dee do!"

"The Fat Brothers!" cried the parson, throwing himself on the ground. "God have mercy on my soul! You can't let them have me!"

"Shut up," said the Horse Girl.

A tall, thin man sauntered casually out of the mist. He wore loose-fitting cotton trousers tied at his waist with a length of rope, but neither shirt nor shoes. His feet were black and his sunken chest laced with scars. On his head, he wore a broad-brimmed straw hat and his eyes were hidden behind dark reflective spectacles. He was grinning as he nonchalantly flipped a knife from one hand to the other.

"How dee do, parson," he said again. He tossed the knife back and forth, back and forth. "Didn't expect we'd meet again so soon."

Around the other side of the circle, another figure emerged from the fog—this one was tall and fat, no shirt, no shoes, head shaved but for a braided queue swinging behind him. He also wore reflective spectacles.

"How dee do, parson," said the fat man.

A third figure emerged from the mist: a short, hunched man wearing a tattered tangzhuang that trailed to the ground. He wore a burlap sack over his head and tied fast around his neck, with two ragged holes torn for his eyes. His finger nails, long and curled talons, extended from the cuffs of his sleeves and dragged along the ground to his sides.

He didn't say anything, but coughed wetly. His burlap sack was stained with red discharge.

"Y'all seem to know each other," said the Horse Girl. "That leaves me the odd one out."

"They call me Auspicious Ed," said the man in the straw hat, "and this here's my brother, Honorable Steve, and my other brother, Inscrutable Joe. We all have long acquaintance with your friend there, though we ain't ever laid eyes on you before, ma'am. You must be new to these parts."

Auspicious Ed sauntered slowly around the circle, always clockwise, flipping his knife from hand to hand, as if searching for a weak spot, while Honorable Steve across from him did the same but widdershins. Inscrutable Joe stood back and coughed.

"What y'all want?"

"We want your friend there, ma'am. That's all. We got matters to discuss. You seen that little church of his? It is still around, ain't it, parson?"

The parson didn't respond—he was too busy mumbling prayers—so the Horse Girl spoke for him. "Yeah, it's still there. I seen it."

"We built that church for him, the three of us together. We had a contract. Now it's time the parson pays us what he owes."

"What's he owe?"

Auspicious Ed looked to his brothers. "Well. For the church, three dollars."

The Horse Girl looked at the parson. "You stiffed these guys three dollars? What the hell kinda church man are you?"

"You don't understand!" cried the parson. "They were heathens! It wasn't a sin!"

"Shit." She looked down at the parson with fresh disgust. "I reckon a man oughta pay his debts. You make a deal with heathens, you pay them heathens."

"Ah!" said Auspicious Ed. "But, see, there's an additional charge."

"What's this additional charge?" said the Horse Girl suspiciously.

"See, after we built that church, we came to collect our fee. Only the parson wasn't there. He had his friend come in his stead. The Hangin' Judge."

"Shit." The Horse Girl wrinkled her nose. The parson continued to wail, tears streaming down his soft cheeks. "I thought you said you ain't had dealings with the Hangin' Judge since you brokered that deal."

"They're heathens! It's no sin!"

"Sounds to me like you and the Hangin' Judge was much closer than you let on. So what's the full story, parson? He came to you to summon the devil and get himself life everlasting…and in return? He gives you the land, he gives you the money. You hire these fine gentlemen to build you a church and, instead of paying them, you let the Judge handle that too? What did he do to you, fellers?"

Auspicious Ed reached up and removed his straw head; the top of his skull was caved in and oozing red. "We don't have quarrel with you, ma'am. So you just push that parson out here, just right across that circle, and we'll be on our way." He grinned, replacing his hat on his head.

The parson flung himself at the Horse Girl's feet, grabbing at the hem of her poncho and wailing louder than ever. "You can't let them have me! It wasn't my fault! The Hangin' Judge said… He tricked me! He said it was fine to do! He said they were heathens, it didn't count!"

"I reckon you're the man of the book, parson. You oughta know what the Lord says about payin' debts. Don't know why you'd be turning to an earthly judge to rule on matters like that."

The parson wailed louder still, somehow, but the Horse Girl was too distracted to pay him any mind. At first, she didn't want to believe what she was seeing. But she couldn't deny the reality facing her.

"Shit. How the hell are you sidewinders doin' that?"

"Doin' what?" said Auspicious Ed innocently. "We ain't doin' nothing. Are we, brothers?"

"Nothing at all," said Honorable Steve.

Inscrutable Joe coughed wetly.

"What!? What is it?" cried the parson.

The Horse Girl pointed to the marks in the dust. "They're shrinkin' the circle. I don't know how they're doing it, but they're doing it."

Indeed, with every rotation, the circle seemed to contract, growing smaller and smaller. The Fat Brothers couldn't cross the line, but it wouldn't take long before the circle would be too small to contain both Horse Girl and parson, and then the Fat Brothers wouldn't have to cross the line at all.

"Shit, shit, shit," said the Horse Girl. She dropped the casket to the ground and pulled back the latches. "I thought we'd have more time, parson, but that ain't a luxury we got no more. We gotta do this now."

"Do what? What's this all about?"

"We gotta do what I brought you along to do. You're a man of God, right? Ya know how to do a baptism?"

"Of course I know how to do a baptism!" huffed the parson indignantly. He was so offended by the insinuation that he forgot to be frightened for a moment.

The Horse Girl shoved her canteen into his hands and pulled back the lid of the casket. The parson stared at what was revealed within.

"Good God," he whispered. And then, as he understood the full horror of the vision before him, he cried out louder: "Good God almighty!"

"I need you to baptize it," said the Horse Girl. "It ain't no good without a soul, parson. Say the words."

"I can't—I can't baptize that! It's an abomination!"

"Baptize it right now, parson, or so help me I'll push you outta this circle and let the Fat Brothers have their way with ya!"

"Yes," said Auspicious Ed, "Do that. Push him out right now."

"We're ready to play," said Honorable Steve.

"This is evil," said the parson. "You'll be damned you, Horse Girl, mark my words! You can't play with something like this—"

"Parson, you ain't in no position to give no sermon. You say the words or we're done here."

The parson paused only for a moment. He looked at the Horse Girl with hate, perhaps the first time in his soft milk-fed life that he ever had felt true burning hate for anything. Even when he was exterminating all them heathens, he never felt hate—pity? Maybe. Disgust? Certainly. But never hate.

The Hangin' Judge had never asked him to betray his faith like this. Of all the sins that he committed in the Judge's service, he had never had to do that. What the Horse Girl asked…

He hated her for asking it.

But the Fat Brothers were waiting impatiently. And the parson decided that being an alive blasphemer was better than being among the righteous dead.

He dropped to his knees and said the words, quietly, under his breath, as if he didn't want God to hear them, didn't want God to hear that he was saying these holy words over *that*, didn't want God to know that he was giving the gift that the Lord had reserved for people to *that*. He tipped the canteen once for the Father, once for the Son, and a third time for the Holy Spirit. The thing in the casket gurgled quietly and, when the rite was complete, the Horse Girl closed the casket again, shut the latches, and hoisted it up on her back.

"Thank you kindly, parson." Then to the Fat Brothers she said, "I don't got no beef with you three. I'm gonna step out of the circle and take my leave. What y'all wanna do with the parson, that's your business."

"You can't leave me to die! You said—!"

"I'm not leaving you to die. You'll be safe as long as you stay inside the circle."

"You can't do this! As a Christian, I beseech you—"

"Seems like justice to me, parson. Ain't right for a man to walk out on his debts."

"Then have mercy! For pity's sake, have mercy! As a Christian!"

"I ain't your god," said the Horse Girl. "That mercy ain't mine to give. So if you want mercy, padre…" She tilted her eyes skyward for a fraction of a second. "Then I suggest you get back to prayin' now."

The parson started to say something but thought better of it. "Leave me the stick! At least leave me the stick!" he cried, pointing at the manzanita branch now lying outside the circle.

"You got as much power in your fingerbone as you got in that stick," said the Horse Girl. "It's just up to you to use it."

She hefted the casket and walked off into the mist. The Fat Brothers stepped aside as she crossed the threshold and they did not stop her. She heard the parson yelling for the next mile, but eventually his wailing stopped. Maybe he got tired. Maybe she simply passed out of range.

Whatever the case, she didn't pause to think any more on the matter. Her goal was set. The Hangin' Judge was ahead and she was ready to meet him now.

5. The Adversary

Santa Diablo was just a few dusty streets lined with snake oil vulcanizing facilities and horse paste grinderies, smokestacks towering above the gray wooden frames of the factories and belching black smoke into the sky. Beyond them, Sugar & Sache could see an endless expanse of snake oil derricks pumping, pumping, pumping. The men, stumbling from their shifts in the factories to their shifts in the taverns, their faces smeared with grime and horse offal, gave her strange looks as she passed, but no one stopped to hassle her. Anyone in this town would be one of the Judge's men. He owned this town, and even these men, who spent their days waist-deep in horse-puree until the smell leaked from their very pores, who smelled so vile that not even the prostitutes who worked the snake oil fields would touch them, who hungered for the touch of a woman above all else, would not dare to delay the Judge's wife as she went about her business.

Even if they didn't recognize her on sight from the cleanliness of her clothes, which they did, she was followed, at a respectable distance, by the two most dangerous members of the Judge's posse, the McCready twins. They were officially tasked with ensuring her safety whenever she left the Judge's villa. But Sugar & Sache knew their real job was to watch her, to make sure she didn't try anything. What would she try? Escape? There was no place for her to go now that the great herds of the Plains were gone. As far as she was concerned, there was nothing out there beyond Santa Diablo.

But she couldn't get Gabby's warnings out of her head. *The Horse Girl is coming.*

Sugar & Sache paused before a rowhouse with a shingle out front—*Physician & Surgeon*—and turned to face her chaperones. "You two wait here."

Butch McCready spat on the ground. "Judge says we gotta stay with ya, ma'am."

"I'm just going to the Doc," said Sugar & Sache.

"Judge says we—"

"It's for my monthlies," said Sugar & Sache with a slight edge in her voice, more than she intended, but enough that the McCready twins reacted. Butch grinned toothlessly and touched the brim of their bowler hat in a gesture that Sugar & Sache couldn't parse, but Femme put a hand on their twin's shoulder that indicated *wait*. The two of them waited as Sugar & Sache ducked into the entryway, through the office, out a doorway in back, and down a flight of stairs, around a corner, then a pause to peer through the alleyway to confirm that, yes, the McCready twins were waiting patiently and obliviously, and then she scampered down the back way.

Only a few houses down, the patent wagons were refueling at the closest snake oil depot, hoses jammed up their sphincters. The wagon at the front of the line was the one she needed, the brightly painted Conestoga with the *Hornswaggle's Patented Brines, Tinctures, and Unguents! Good for What Ails you!* marquee. A little man was out front, arranging a pyramid of green glass bottles, each filled with thick black liquid.

"Sir? Sir?"

He turned and she found herself looking down at a short plump little man wearing a dapper black suit and a stovepipe hat that was substantially taller than he was. His bushy handlebar mustache twitched above a cheerful grin almost too wide for his face. Sugar & Sache could see herself reflected in his dark spectacles. His clothes were too clean and his face too soft to be a snake oil refinery worker or a horse paste grinder.

"Sir, are you…are you *him*?"

"Him? Him? Madam, you have the advantage of me!" said the little man, slapping himself on the forehead. "I am no other, as you can see from my sign—the name's Herr Doktor Professor Ulysses P. Hornswaggle, PhD, MD, DoD. My card!" He pulled a card from his vest and held it out to Sugar & Sache with a flourish, but she did not take it.

"I don't have time for a snake oil pitch today, sir," said Sugar & Sache.

"Oh, you injure me, madam!" cried the little man. "To accuse me of being, what, some kind of mercenary salesman? No, no, nothing could be further from the truth—"

"I don't have any money for a snake oil pitch either, sir."

The little man paused. "Well, now that, *that* might be a bigger problem. But you've pulled on my heartstrings, madam, I simply can't bear to see a lady in distress. Please, take it! It's yours! Absolutely free of charge!"

The little man slapped a little vial into Sugar & Sache's hand before she had a chance to protest. She looked down at the green bottle in the palm of her hand.

"Hornswaggle's Patented Cure-All Unguent!" The little man tipped his stovepipe hat. "Good for rickets, hydrophobia, and juggler's malaise! Made of 100% guaranteed snake oil! Just so happens that the good people of Santa Diablo have a powerful need for healthful tonics and brews. Why, my good lady, did you know that there was a terrible outbreak of the intangible squirms just last year? And over eight reported cases of buzzard craw fever? It's never been more clear to me that a town was ever in such dire need of my marvelous medicines to restore vigor and stamina!"

"I don't need this. I need to ask—the people are talking… Is the Horse Girl on the move?"

Hornswaggle looked her up and down as if seeing her for the first time. His mustache twitched again.

"I know who you are," said Sugar & Sache. "I've seen you hanging around town. Keeping an eye on your investment."

Hornswaggle pushed his reflective spectacles down his nose and fixed Sugar & Sache with eyes suddenly revealed to be the golden color of egg yolks. His pupils were not round, but rather long and rectangular like the pupils of a goat.

"Well, madam, that's just good business sense, wouldn't you say? Yes, you've discovered me, good show, madam! I've had a long association with your husband, after all. You do know about your husband's past, don't you? I should hate to think that the estimable Judge Lazarus Dives is one of those men who tries to hide his past from his very wife, the one person with whom he should be the most open and honest? I understand our Judge Dives was quite the rascal in his younger days, a regular roughriding outlaw, you might say! The Dives gang robbed stagecoaches and banks all across the state and Johnny Law just couldn't catch them! They were so notorious that they said Dives himself sold his soul to the devil for immortality…so no law man could shoot him down and no noose could hang him!"

Sugar & Sache didn't know the Judge in those days. She only remembered him as far back as the day that he appeared on the horizon, a black silhouette against the red prairie sun, his duster flapping in the wind like the wings of a great bat. She remembered the men who came with him, how they rounded up the horses, cracking their whips and firing their pistols. She remembered the great combine harvester, bigger than a barn, a massive city-sized mechanical monster on rails, its open mouth like the maw of some great whale scooping up everything in its path and the churning blades and the hose in back that sprayed 100% pure, unadulterated horse paste into tanks as big as buffalo carcasses. She remembered when the Judge appeared to her, looming above her, looking down at her, her and the Horse Girl, the last of the great herd, these two sisters, inseparable, and the Judge laughed deep in his throat, a laugh she would never forget, a laugh she sometimes heard her husband still make in his sleep, and he offered them a choice. He offered it to each of them. And Sugar & Sache chose holy matrimony, chose the Judge's bed over the grinding of the machine, and now here she was. No one could hold it against her. Who would have chosen different?

"I don't need a lecture," said Sugar & Sache. "How is the Horse Girl coming? I saw it with my own eyes. I saw the Judge put her in the machine."

Hornswaggle shrugged. "Couldn't say, madam. La Muerte must have sent her back. Not my place to say why,

I never could understand that woman's logic. She probably done it to get back at me, honestly. She's mighty sore about that little deal I made with your husband, I reckon."

"I want to make a deal," said Sugar & Sache.

Hornswaggle laughed. "Ha! What a kidder you are! A nice gal like you? Making trouble for the Judge? Ha ha! Now that's a great gag! Why would you want to do that?"

"Send the Horse Girl away. Anywhere. I don't care where. Just…make her not come here."

"Why, not excited to see your sister?" said Hornswaggle, clucking his tongue in mock sympathy. "I should think you'd be happy to be reunited! There was a time when the two of you were inseparable." He caught sight of something out of the corner of his eye and shouted angrily. "Echidna! You get back inside!"

Sugar & Sache looked to see a young girl with pigtails and a gingham dress leaning out of the wagon. Like Hornswaggle, she had gold eyes and rectangular pupils. At Hornswaggle's command, she ducked back inside.

Hornswaggle shook his head. "Kids!"

"Your daughter?"

"Granddaughter, actually. Don't got no daughter, never had one. Not entirely sure why, actually. It's just one of those things, where you have a granddaughter but no daughter. Sorta like having a grandmother but no mother, ya know? It's the darndest thing! But we were speaking business, weren't we? Now I could do what you ask me, madam, I could. But I'm a man of business, you see, so I'm obligated to ask: What's in it for me?"

"Anything! Anything you want!"

"Madam, you don't have anything I want."

"My soul! You could have it! Please, if you'll just make the Horse Girl go away." Sugar & Sache's voice cracked; she was trying to maintain her composure, but she could feel herself breaking. She couldn't face the Horse Girl. She couldn't stand for the Horse Girl to see her now, what she was now, what she had become, the kept woman of the Hangin' Judge, the consort to the man who had killed their family, their herd, their entire way of life… The Horse Girl who was also given the same choice, who made the choice that Sugar & Sache couldn't. The Horse Girl knew she was a traitor and a coward, and the Horse Girl was coming. The Horse Girl was coming to kill the Judge and collect the bounty, and what the Horse Girl planned to do to Sugar & Sache she had no idea—the reality was that it didn't matter. She couldn't bear for the Horse Girl to see her, to look into her eyes, to know that Sugar & Sache had chosen to live while the Horse Girl had chosen to die.

Hornswaggle grinned and tipped his stovepipe hat politely. "Madam, with all due respect, that ain't yours to sell anymore. You've already made that deal with another."

Sugar & Sache squinted into the distance. At the north end of town, beyond the bobbing snake oil derricks, the Judge's stately Italianate villa loomed on the horizon. Three floors of the finest in luxury living west of the Mississippi. Indoor plumbing. Gas lighting. Fifteen-foot ceilings. And a tower with a sun room and widow's walk. The Judge had spared no expense. Sugar & Sache had a good life there. She was first among his wives, so she had run of the house while the Judge was away, which was often, and the terrified respect of the townspeople. The Judge rarely imposed on her. Rarely. So rarely that she really shouldn't complain. She was alive, after all. It could have been different.

Better to live in a house than a muddy old field. That's what she always told herself.

Hornswaggle was talking, more to himself now than to her, but she wasn't listening. "I suppose I should have expected she'd put out that bounty, she never has been very happy about this particular deal. Seems to feel like it's treading on her feet or something, but, really, it's just a little mutual agreement between two consenting parties that shouldn't involve her at all! Well, maybe it did impede on her territory just a tad… Nevertheless, the deed is done! So even if the Horse Girl does come I must ask, what does she intend to do about it? She must know that she can't hope to stand against the Judge. Our contract is ironclad."

A dry wind whipped through her hair. She needed to get back. The McCready twins would only wait so long before they started to get suspicious.

"We'll see," said Sugar & Sache.

6. The Hangin' Judge

There were men squatting on the porch of the Judge's house and, judging from their general demeanor, the Horse Girl did not take them for common laborers. These were men of violence. She could see it in their eyes when they looked at her, the same delight that she saw in the eyes of the Fat Brothers when they spied the parson out in the Bone Yard. These were men who lived in violence the way a fish lives in water.

"What you want, girl?" said one, a big hairy man with an eyepatch over his left-most eye. "This here's private property."

"Hospitality," said the Horse Girl, who had lingered in the shadows for days since her arrival in Santa Diablo and watched the lawyers approach the Judge's house. They always cited the same sacred right so that the Judge's posse would allow them entry, and now the Horse Girl aped their behavior in hopes that it would also work for her. She tensed, her fingers hovering above her holstered six-shooter, ready to draw, but the men on the porch only exchanged annoyed glances.

"You a lawyer?" said the hairy man. "You don't look like no lawyer."

"I invoke hospitality," repeated the Horse Girl. "Y'all have a problem with that?"

"You leave your gun here, missy," said the hairy man.

The Horse Girl grimaced but she pulled her six-shooter and threw it to the floor. Another man, a tall spindly man with a twitchy nose and buck teeth, swooped forward and took it. After that, the men parted and allowed the Horse Girl to ascend the front steps and enter the Judge's house.

She had come so far—breaching the Church of the Last Redoubt, bringing the parson to the Cantina at the Cross Roads, crossing the Bone Yard, facing the Fat Brothers, traveling to Santa Diablo, and now had made it. Now the Horse Girl sat in the foyer of Judge Lazarus Dives' Italianate villa, clutching her casket to her chest and waiting for her audience with the man himself.

Men sat in chairs along the wall to the left and to the right of her, each one with his hat on his knees and a leather satchel at his feet. Periodically, a woman with a tight bun of hair and cat-eye spectacles would enter from the parlor and call the name of a man, who would rise and follow her into the parlor. Sometime after, that man would leave with a miserable look on his face and the woman would call another man in. There were other women around as well, lounging in doorways and giggling with the men still seated. All the women were in various states of undress and every woman wore cat-eye spectacles and hair tightly tied into a bun. One woman walked along the line, a clipboard in hand, peering at each man in turn over the rims of her spectacles.

"Business?" she asked one man and then another. They were each of them here to plead a case in front of the Judge, but the Horse Girl did not get the impression that a one of them had representation. When the woman approached the Horse Girl, her question was different.

"Young lady, are you here to audition for the Judge's bed?" she said, pushing her glasses up over the bridge of her nose and arching a finely painted eyebrow. "Sit up straight! You'll never amount to anything with posture like that."

The Horse Girl glared at the woman and did not adjust her posture. The woman frowned. A second woman, her ample chest bare and her nipples erect, bounced into place beside the first. She carried a yardstick.

"Is there a problem, Miss Marplethorpe?"

"Not at all, Miss Nettleweb," said the first. "I was merely instructing this young lady on proper posture."

"Mmm, of course, of course," said the second. "If I may, Miss Marplethorpe? With today's young people, one needs a firm hand. Allow me to demonstrate."

To the Horse Girl, she yelled: "You there! None of this slacking!" She cracked the yardstick across the Horse Girl's lap with enough vigor that the Horse Girl leapt to her feet.

"What the hell?!"

"Perfect, perfect. You see, Miss Marplethorpe, how the student now gives me her full attention. Let that be a lesson to you."

"Yes, Miss Nettleweb. Thank you, Miss Nettleweb."

Miss Nettleweb peered over her spectacles at the Horse Girl, imitating the pose of her fellow. "Business?"

"Gonna kill the Judge," said the Horse Girl. The women exchanged glances and the one wrote something on her clipboard, but neither of them seemed especially concerned. Doubtless the Horse Girl was not the first assassin to visit the Judge at home. He must trust his bargain to protect him.

"You, to the head of the line," said Miss Marplethorpe. "Go on, go on! Let's get this over with."

The Horse Girl rose from her seat, the men surrounding her staring with envy or possibly pity. The two women herded her out of the foyer and into the parlor, where, seated on a towering rattan throne among towering stacks of yellowed legal paperwork thick with dust and festooned with cobwebbing, sat the Judge Lazarus Dives in all his infernal glory.

The Horse Girl hesitated only a moment. It had been a long time since she had seen him, so many years that she wasn't sure that she would recognize his face anymore, but she did. Those features were burned into her memory. He was a giant of a man, so tall that his head nearly touched the ceiling and so massive that he barely fit into his rattan peacock chair. Even in his advancing years, his ropey physique and snowy white horseshoe mustache and long white hair remained striking. His thick neck was twice ringed with purple scars, reminders of the law's two unsuccessful attempts to deal with him before he became the law. He wore an expertly tailored white cotton suit. A nude woman stood next to him, sliding papers under his pen for him to sign. The nude woman also had cat-eye glasses and a severe bun.

"So you know enough to invoke hospitality," said the Judge, not looking up. "That tells me you're either a lawyer or smart enough to pretend to be one."

"I come to—"

"Did the Judge invite you to speak?" said the nude woman harshly, glaring at the Horse Girl over the rims of her glasses. "If you have something to say, a polite young woman raises her hand, thank you very much!"

"We don't need to stand on formalities here," said the Judge, replacing his pen in its inkwell. He rolled up this latest document and handed it back to the nude woman. "Eunice, please take this to the boys out front. That'll be all."

Eunice bowed her head and left the room.

"I hope my wives didn't cause you too much distress," said the Judge, glancing up from his papers for only a moment before he returned to his work. "I tell them not to harass my guests, but old habits die hard for them, I'm afraid."

"Are all your wives schoolmarms?"

"Most of them. Call it a personal failing, but I find myself unable to resist the lure of a delectable schoolmarm in all her restrained, buttoned-down majesty. There are men who love blondes and others who love redheads, but give me a good schoolmarm with just the lightest streaking of gray in that mousey brown bun any day of the week. And, of course, I don't need to tell you that your average schoolmarm is absolute dynamite in the sack. It's all that sublimated energy, you see; they keep such a tight lid on themselves in the classroom that they just *have* to let it out somewhere. But you didn't come here to discuss my taste in women, did you? What is it that I can do for you, Miss…?"

"I'm here to kill you," said the Horse Girl.

The Judge put down his papers, suddenly interested in the Horse Girl for the first time. "Now that would be a sight. Lots of folks come to me with that goal, but ain't a one that's accomplished it yet. You can take your shot and suffer the consequences, or you can turn tail and leave. I'm a fair man, I won't send my posse after you. You can go back to where ever you came from and we can forget any of this ever happened. Then again…"

The Judge settled back in his chair, the wicker squeaking as he shifted his weight. He looked at her with keen interest.

"Then again, there's something about you that makes me think you ain't the sort that can just go home and forget. I reckon you came a long way. And you're traveling a road that can only end with one of us dead. Am I right?"

"You're a lotta things, Judge, but you ain't no fool."

"Now then," said the Judge, resting his scruffy chin against one gigantic knuckle. "You've piqued my interest. Who are you? What are you? I thought I was familiar with all the breeds of Indian there were out here in Alta California. But you, my dear, you stump me. Chumash, perhaps? Pomo? Or are you from above Santa Diablo? Perhaps Maidu?"

"I ain't from Alta California," said the Horse Girl. "I'm from the Plains."

"Ah! Pawnee, then?"

"I ain't Indian," said the Horse Girl. "I'm bay."

"Bay? Of course!" He snapped his fingers in sudden recognition. "You're the Horse Girl! I heard you were back. How you're back, I simply cannot fathom—but that's a question I'll leave for the scientists to answer. My goodness, then I have something you simply must see. Follow me, please."

The Judge rose from his chair, stretched briefly so that his hands nearly brushed the ceiling beams, and then motioned for the Horse Girl to follow as he began down a hallway.

"Let me show you something," said the Judge. "I think you'll find this most curious. The prize of my collection! Now, you remember our last meeting, that was back when I was in the horse paste trade. I can imagine you find the whole process distasteful, but the high society ladies of Boston and Philadelphia need food for their precious kitties—and they're willing to pay top dollar for it too! I was the first to round up the bounty of the prairie— the buffalo, the gazelle, the mustang—for this most lucrative purpose! But while I was thus engaged, I found a most interesting specimen. Won't you take a look?"

The Judge opened the door into the kitchen. A woman at the stove turned around at their entrance. Her face was white and brown with a little dab of orange between her eyes, which widened when she caught sight of the Horse Girl.

"The Horse Girl!" cried Sugar & Sache, dropping her skillet to the floor so that the fried eggs splattered into explosions of sizzling yellow goo.

"Sugar & Sache!" cried the Horse Girl.

Sugar & Sache whinnied. The Horse Girl whinnied back, unable to control herself. The Horse Girl took a step forward, but Sugar & Sache, eyes still wide, vibrated her head just the slightest bit to indicate: *No. Please. Stay back.*

The Horse Girl saw and understood and she stayed back. But it was too late.

"You remember each other, do you?" said the Judge. "Good to see your trip through the machine didn't affect your memory. I reckon you came back for her?"

The Horse Girl steeled herself. This was something that she did not expect. But she was not to be deterred from her purpose. "She ain't my sister. I don't care a whit for that traitor. I came back to kill you, Judge."

"Not your sister, no? But she is my wife. And I must say, we've been very happy together. Isn't that right, Sugar & Sache?"

Sugar & Sache lowered her face. Why was he making her say it? It was hard enough to say when they were alone, when the only people who had to hear the lie were herself and the Judge. But to say it in front of the Horse Girl…

"Isn't that right, Sugar & Sache?"

Sugar & Sache looked at the Judge, begging him with her eyes. *Don't make me say it. Please. Don't make me say it.*

But the Judge looked back and there was nothing but murder in his pale blue eyes.

"Yes," said Sugar & Sache quietly. "We've been very happy."

"Much better to live in a house than out in a muddy old field, don't you think?" said the Judge. "Wouldn't you say, Horse Girl, that my Sugar & Sache is oh so fortunate to marry a man such as me who can give her anything that she desires?"

"You put her herd through the processor," said the Horse Girl. "You put *our* herd through the processor."

"Don't be so sentimental," said the Judge. "They were just horses."

"Just horses!" repeated the Horse Girl. "Just horses!"

The Judge rolled his blue eyes. "Come now, Horse Girl. I was there when the ninth cavalry slaughtered the last of the Pombo at Weeping Rock. I once saw a San Francisco mob tear apart a dozen Chinamen over a spent snake oil claim. You would think such sights would move people to tears, but I've never seen tears shed like when those horses dropped into the grinder. People really do think them magnificent animals, don't they? Nevertheless, commerce must happen."

"You mother fucker," said the Horse Girl. "You goddamn mother fucker!"

The Judge smiled benignly. "I'm sorry you don't feel the same way, Horse Girl. But your feelings, as it were, are irrelevant."

"I'll kill you! I'll kill you right here, right now!" snarled the Horse Girl, tugging at the releases on her leather straps and allowing the casket to clatter to the ground.

"There's no need for theatrics," said the Judge. "You must understand, Horse Girl, I've heard all this before. Surely you don't think that you're the only jilted husband to walk through my doors? Why, every one of my schoolmarms, and I do love them all dearly, was once someone's wife! So many angry husbands, all shouting and yelling and waving around their guns and making big ol' promises that I was gonna pay for this. Oh my, how they loved to say that! Some of them tried to take me to court, a fool's gambit you might say, as *I am* the court. The ones who took direct action, well, those I can almost forgive for thinking it might work."

"I know about the deal," said the Horse Girl, now fumbling with the latches. "I know what you sold to Old Scratch and I know what he gave ya for it."

Sugar & Sache stepped back, pressing herself against the wall, her chest fluttering in terror, whickering so fearfully that foam gathered at the corners of her mouth.

"Oh, excellent. Marvelous! Then you already know: I cannot be killed by any man born of woman. And please, before you embarrass yourself with quibbles, I know that you are no man. Don't you think I would have anticipated such a thing? A man of the law such as myself getting caught by a mere legal technicality? Oh, that is rich, Horse Girl, very rich." The Judge chuckled and then frowned, looking down at the Horse Girl on the floor where she struggled with the latches on her casket. "Whatever are you doing down there?"

"Shut up! I ain't gonna shoot ya! He is."

The Horse Girl threw open the casket and revealed what was inside.

The casket was entirely filled with roots, strung and restrung back and forth across the width and breadth of the interior, filling every iota of space until the casket's interior was nothing but a single twisted mass of tendrils.

The tendrils waved and twitched, sensing the open air, and started to send up sprouts.

The men outside had confiscated her six-shooter, but she extended her arm and a tiny derringer dropped from her sleeve. It was a small gun with only four rounds. They would have to count. The Horse Girl held it out. "Take it, Lil' Varmint!"

A new sapling grew up and through the trigger guard and around the barrel, slowly pulling the pistol from the Horse Girl's hands and bending to aim it toward the judge.

"What in the hell?" screamed the Judge.

The branches were twisting, binding, coalescing, until the creature was almost human-shaped, waving its branch arm frenetically with the derringer still aimed true.

"It's something, ain't it? That's what the great master alchemist Paracelsus called a Lil' Varmint! Ain't too hard to grow one, just a mandrake root incubated in a vat of horse manure and nourished quarterly with milk and bats' blood. And the best part? He ain't born of woman!"

It took a step, which is to say that the leading tentacles of the homunculus grabbed at the floor, dragging the rootbound casket behind them.

"That ain't possible! How's it got the sense to aim that gun? That ain't possible!"

"Now, the hard part about a Lil' Varmint ain't growin' one," continued the Horse Girl. "The hard part is gettin' it to do anything besides wallow in the muck. It ain't naturally got no more sense than a prickly pear, just wants to eat and sleep. Just like a critter, ya know? Ain't got no soul and ain't got nothin' goin' on upstairs."

She tapped her temple. The Lil' Varmint raised the derringer. Its branches shook – but only because the gun was heavy, not believe its nerve was failing. One look at the Lil' Varmint and there could be no doubt that it was entirely ready to kill. Its movements betrayed something beyond animal cunning, something approaching human reason.

"At least, not 'til it gets the inner light. It's got sense now, 'cause I got it baptized. It's got all the knowledge of good and evil it needs to commit murder!"

"That's an abomination!" roared the Judge. "I ain't even a religious man and I know that! God damn it! You're gonna be damned for making that thing!"

"Then let God damn me," said the Horse Girl. "I seen a lot of folks on my travels. But I ain't never met God yet, so I guess he ain't got that much interest in what I do. Doubt he'll start takin' interest now."

The Lil' Varmint squeezed the trigger. There was a violent explosion and a puff of smoke and a recoil that made the homunculus jump back. The Judge gave a groan and slumped backwards, his hands to his chest, red gushing between his sausage-sized fingers. Sugar & Sache screamed and dropped to her knees. The gunshot reverberated through the rafters and already the Horse Girl could hear the resulting chaos through the door—the schoolmarms in the foyer were shrieking and yelling. She heard feet slapping against steps; the posse was coming, fighting its way through the escaping crowd of schoolmarms and penitents.

"You son of a bitch!" roared the Judge, jumping back to his feet with fresh excitement. But the expression on his face told it all. Lil' Varmint's aim was true. The Judge was injured. The Judge was capable of being injured. But he was a big man and one bullet wasn't enough. He lurched forward, reaching for the opened casket with murder in his eyes. The Horse Girl pulled it back out of his reach—the Lil' Varmint's arm wobbled and another round discharged impotently into the ceiling.

The kitchen door flew open and Two-Eyed Mulligan filled the doorway; he took a single look at his injured boss and reached for his six-shooter, but the Lil' Varmint had regained its balance and it was quicker on the draw. Mulligan was not as big as the Judge and one bullet was all it took. But there were more men behind him, climbing over his body, fumbling with their six-shooters, and the Lil' Varmint's derringer only had one more round.

"Don't waste 'em on the posse!" shouted the Horse Girl. "I'll hold 'em off! Get the Judge!"

The Horse Girl jumped over the table and slid into the Jackelope, feet first, the man's teeth cracking with a satisfying crunch as she sent him flying. He tumbled backwards into Angelhair Horchata, who dropped his six-shooter in shock. That was enough time for the Horse Girl to get her feet back on the floor. She ran at them, throwing her body into the fray, her hands scrabbling for the dropped gun. She pulled it up in an arc, discharging bullets without thought. One split Skunkface Sally's head open like a melon to spray brains across the kitchen ceiling. Another blasted the Jackelope's hand before he could reach his own six-shooter. In the butler's pantry beyond the kitchen, the Horse Girl could see the McCready twins, pistols already drawn.

Meanwhile, the Judge's enormous boots stomped upon the casket until it busted to splinters, and his massive hands ripped the derringer from the Lil' Varmint's grasp just as the final bullet exploded in his face. The Judge roared in pain and confusion, blinded by the smoke, blood streaming from his forehead. He plunged his hands into the casket, into the eel's nest of branches that was the Lil' Varmint, and pulled it apart, still bellowing, insane with rage that this should happen, that he should be injured so, that someone should dare to do this to him in his own house. But that was when Sugar & Sache rose, still clutching the hot frying pan sticky with molten egg, and swung it to strike the Judge in the face. The Judge's face shattered with a sizzling crack.

"Jesus Christ!" cried the Horse Girl.

The Judge didn't speak. He looked at her, shock written across his ruined face. Sugar & Sache, who had shared his bed, who had quietly accepted all the humiliations he had visited upon her, who did not complain because she knew what it meant to complain and she knew how much worse it could be if she complained. Who knew she had a good deal with the Judge and there would be nothing better for her than that. She was the one who had struck him.

Sugar & Sache pulled the pan back, tearing skin, clotting blood sizzling into a red crust, and swung again, harder. The Judge collapsed to his knees and then flat on his face. Sugar & Sache continued to bring the pan down upon his head, again and again, until the Judge's skull was smashed into a slurry of hair and blood and bits of egg. She only stopped after many long minutes. She stood, looking down at her creation, wheezing with the effort, still clutching the pan which continued to sizzle.

She looked at the Horse Girl. The Horse Girl looked back. The Horse Girl stared at the carcass in confusion. The Judge was dead, although he shouldn't be.

7. A Good Day for a Hanging

The mystery of the Judge's death would continue to puzzle the people of Alta California for years to come, since it was well known that he could not be killed by any man born of woman. Some wags, of course, pointed to the obvious conclusion, that neither the Horse Girl nor Sugar & Sache were men and (there was considerable disagreement in the press about which of the two women had ultimately swung the fatal frying pan) thus the Judge was done in by a quibble, but others insisted that the Judge, being a man of the law, would never have fallen for such an obvious loophole. Unfortunately, the only person who could definitively settle the issue had packed up his medicine wagon that very morning, as if he had advance warning of the events to come, and departed Santa Diablo for parts unknown.

Now there was the business of justice to be done.

The governor of Alta California was a small, squat man with a thin mustache upon his lip and a bowler hat that he continuously twirled nervously in his hands. No one in the crowd remembered him, since before this day his only business in Santa Diablo was the annual visit to pay fealty to the Judge and to beg for campaign donations. But that day he had another duty; he had to oversee a hanging, although the actual mechanics of the act were being overseen by various schoolmarms. The schoolmarms, in general, had taken command since the fateful day that the Horse Girl and Sugar & Sache, vile accomplices in perfidy, had murdered the Judge. It was Miss Nettleweb, after a battlefield promotion to first wife, who placed the noose around the neck of the Horse Girl.

"Do you have any last words, Horse Girl?" said Miss Nettleweb as she primly adjusted the rope. The Horse Girl glared at her, but remained silent.

"A proper lady responds when she is asked a question," said Miss Nettleweb archly, but the Horse Girl simply off stared into the distance, watching the snake oil derricks pumping, pumping. The Judge was dead, but the derricks kept going. The death of one man, even a man as powerful as Judge Lazarus Dives, was not enough to warrant a pause in extraction. The new world required snake oil.

It was a new world that the Horse Girl wouldn't witness. That was fine. She was done with it. She'd done what she came to do. She'd done the one thing that kept her going. She was done.

Sugar & Sache was crying next to her, less serene in her fate.

"Sugar & Sache? Any last words?"

"I didn't mean to do it! I didn't mean it! I shouldn't have done it!" Sugar & Sache couldn't stop her blubbering, fat tears rolling down her cheeks. "It wasn't so bad… I had a good deal…"

The first few rows of audience were entirely schoolmarms, who refrained from jeering only because even in the depths of their rage they felt the need to set a good example—but behind them stood the rank and file of snake oil drillers and horse paste grinders, who hooted and hollered enough to compensate. Over to the side stood the remaining members of the Judge's old posse, frustrated in their new irrelevance, baying for blood as well.

"Sorry about this," said the Horse Girl to Sugar & Sache. "I didn't mean to get you involved. You didn't need to get involved. But if you didn't, I'd be hangin' alone."

Sugar & Sache sniffled harder.

The Horse Girl squinted into the distance. The jeering crowd was a smear of faces, a blur of noise. "If nothin' else, I prefer some company, sister."

Sugar & Sache nodded. "Sister."

Someone pulled the switch, the floor beneath their feet fell away, and the two sisters dropped sharply into oblivion.

"Well, Horse Girl," said the La Muerte. "I told you our next meeting would be our last."

She dropped a burlap sack upon the table top with a jangling thud. Under the table, an old black moggy stirred to life at the sound, briefly glanced up to note that she was no longer alone in the room, and slunk away to find a more secluded hiding spot. Sugar & Sache looked about, taking in her surroundings for the first time. She could hear laughter and music through the walls and smell something hot and delicious cooking on a stove.

"Told you I'd make good," said the Horse Girl. "What're you gonna do with the Judge?"

"That's none of your concern."

The Horse Girl paused then jerked her head toward Sugar & Sache. "What about her? It wasn't fair. It wasn't supposed to go like that. I just got her mixed up in it."

"And yet here she is. She made her choice, Horse Girl, and she's here now. You're both here. That's all there is to it." La Muerte turned to leave, but paused in the doorway, apparently moved to pity. "I'll have them bring you both some coffin varnish while you wait. On the house."

The Judge's villa was three floors of the finest in luxury living west of the Mississippi. Indoor plumbing. Gas lighting. Fifteen-foot ceilings. And a tower with a sun room and widow's walk. Sugar & Sache was first among the wives, and had run of the house when the Judge was out, which was often, and the terrified respect of the town. And all she had to do was keep the Judge happy, to lie in bed and look into the face of the man who had killed her herd and say, "Thank you." He wasn't asking that much, if you thought about it. It was a good deal for her.

And now she was here.

"I'm glad he's dead," said Sugar & Sache suddenly. "Fuck him."

"Fuck him," repeated the Horse Girl. Then she said: "Well. I guess we got some time to kill."

"I guess so," said Sugar & Sache.

They waited for the coffin varnish, and, when it arrived, the sisters drank it together.

ABOUT THE AUTHORS

LYNDSEY CROAL is a Scottish author with work published in over eighty magazines and anthologies, including with *Apex, Flash Fiction Online, Analog,* and *Weird Tales.* She's a Scottish Book Trust New Writers Awardee, British Fantasy Award Finalist, and former Hawthornden Fellow. Her novelette *Have You Decided on Your Question* (2023) and debut short story collection *Limelight and Other Stories* (2024) are published with Shortwave Publishing. Her second collection of Scottish folklore-inspired tales *Dark Crescent* is forthcoming in 2025 from Luna Press. She lives in Edinburgh with her giant kitten Pippin and by day works in climate change policy and comms. She's currently working on other longer projects in the sci-fi and horror space. Find out more via www.lyndseycroal.co.uk.

BITTER KARELLA is a genderfluid transvestite goblin, writer, and creator of the three-time Hugo-nominated microfiction comedy account @Midnight_Pals which asks what if all your favorite horror writers were to gather around the campfire and tell scary stories like in the classic Nickelodeon series "Are You Afraid of the Dark?" Karella writes gonzo psycho-sexual body horror with a grotesquely humorous edge. His short story "Low Tide Jenny," originally published in Seize the Press magazine, was a winner of the Brave New Weird award for best new weird fiction of 2022 by Tenebrous Press. Her work has also appeared in Bag of Bones' "Step into the Light," Tenebrous Press' "Your Body is Not Your Body," Ghoulish Books' "Bound in Flesh," and From Beyond Press' "This World Belongs to Us." She's co-host of the podcast "A Special Presentation, or Alf Will Not be Seen Tonight" about comic strips adapted into TV specials and plays Roger Corman in the "Submitted for the Approval of the Midnight Pals" podcast. Karella lives with their partner, two cats, and a tarantula. When not writing, he also dabbles in text game design.

ABOUT THE ARTISTS

Viviana is a Portuguese artist most known as **ECHO ECHO**. Her creative influence is born in observing nature to the smallest details and recreating that feeling in her illustrations. She likes to create new worlds, bringing some sort of reality to these fantasy worlds while filling them with psychedelic manifestations of her imagination. Find more of her work on Instagram @echoechoillustrations.

EVANGELINE GALLAGHER is an award-winning illustrator from Baltimore, Maryland. They received their BFA in Illustration from the Maryland Institute College of Art in 2018. When they aren't drawing they're probably hanging out with their dog, Charlie, or losing at a board game. They possess the speed and enthusiasm of 10,000 illustrators.

CONTENT WARNINGS

These stories are works of horror fiction which contain dark content that may be triggering to some individuals. In addition to instances and implications of violence and death throughout, there are instances of child neglect and abuse in "The Girl with Barnacles for Eyes." Please read with caution.

TENEBROUS PRESS

aims to drag the malleable Horror genre into newer,
Weirder territory with stories that are incisive,
provocative, intelligent and terrifying; delivered by
voices diverse and unsung.

FIND OUT MORE:
www.tenebrouspress.com
Social Media @TenebrousPress

NEW WEIRD HORROR